Steeple Hills Chronicle:

Unrest In Peace

By

Joseph Lagano

1
New Arrival

A quiet and gentle autumn breeze blew through Main Street stretching across Steeple Hills, Maine. Brown and orange leaves painted the streets and sidewalks, some danced around the lampposts as the wind blew them around. The townspeople bustled about, some carrying pumpkins, others carrying lights and scarecrows.

As the wind carried the brisk autumn breeze, a silver car rode down Main Street. Its wheels dirty with mud, little rocks stuck in the treads. It stopped in front of the town hall, a brick building and the second tallest building in town. The front door was large and dark red, stone trimming outlined the front door, at the very top of the door was a carving that read…EST 1813.

Wendy Carlyle sat behind the wheel. She wore a collared long-sleeved black shirt that slightly hung over a pair of jeans that barely touched her black sneakers. She sighed with relief that the drive from New York City was over. It was meant to be an eight-hour drive, but thanks to several New England traffic jams, the drive took almost twenty hours, a drive that cost her a big gulp, a purchase she would come to regret.

She wasn't alone in the car; her daughter Elsa slept in the passenger seat. A black leather jacket draped over her like a blanket. Sunglasses covered Elsa's eyes; her black hair tied in a ponytail. One headphone lounging on her shoulder, the other dangling from her ear. "Time to wake up kiddo." Wendy said gently shaking her daughter's shoulder. Elsa squirmed a little before waking up and stretching out her arms, nearly hitting her mother in the face.

"We're here?" she asked, a bit groggy.

"Yeah. Finally. Get on out and stretch your legs." She and Elsa both got out of the car. Elsa put on her jacket, covering her ratty orange t-shirt. The shirt had black markings on it, almost looking like a jack-o-lantern. Elsa stretched her legs that seemed comfy in a pair of blue jeans that stopped just before her dirty white sneakers, the stretching felt beyond heavenly.

Elsa leaned back against the car while Wendy stood up straight. "I think I might've run over a screw back there during,"

"I still don't get why we moved here." Elsa said, ignoring her mother.

"Ellie…"

"Elsa. No one has called me Ellie since I was ten." Elsa corrected her mother, rather coldly. Wendy sighed,

"We had to get out of the city. It wasn't the best environment for you." Wendy said.

"So, you wait until I'm a sophomore in High School. I'll be gone in two years. Smart move." Wendy rolled her eyes; she wasn't the biggest fan of Elsa's sarcasm. But wished Elsa would grow to love this town just as Wendy did growing up.

"All we need is the deed to the house,"

"I'm staying with the car." Elsa stated, preferring to continue to stretch her legs than walk up the ten steps to get into town hall.

"Ok." Wendy said, rolling her eyes again. "I'll be right back." Elsa shrugged her shoulders as her mother walked inside. She stood up straight and pulled the purple band out of her hair, letting it drop to her shoulders. Elsa held her sunglasses to her face and shook her head to loosen her hair a bit more. Elsa took a look at the town ahead of her. It looked cozy; small mom and pop shops lined Main Street.

Pumpkins dangled from lampposts, connected by orange and black streamers. Ghost and pumpkin string lights hung from nearly every tree branch. High above, hanging on wires was a giant banner. It was orange with big black writing in a haunting font reading….

Steeple Hills Annual Halloween Festival!

Halloween Night on Main Street, Sundown!

Elsa took out her cell phone, ignoring how low her battery was. She snapped various pictures of the town. "I already hate this town." She said with disgust in her voice. She put her phone in her pocket. A strong wind blew through, sending the leaves flying into Elsa's face. She did her best to swat them away, nearly knocking her sunglasses off and dropping her hairband in the process.

"Excuse me miss." Elsa turned seeing a young man, about her height, holding her hairband. He seemed a bit startled when she turned, he might've been standing too close. He had on blue jeans and black sneakers along with a gray hoodie, which looked to have some dirt on the front pocket. His hair was covered by his hood, but Elsa could see a hint of brown peeking out. But it was his eyes that caught her attention, Puppy dog brown. "I, uh, think you dropped this." Elsa found herself speechless, unusual for her, but she quickly snapped out of it.

"Thanks." She said, taking the hairband back.

The young man fumbled to speak, quickly putting his hands in the pocket of his sweatshirt, though it was starting to rip. "You're - You're welcome. I guess you're new here huh." The boy said, finding the words.

"That obvious?" Elsa asked sarcastically. Again, the boy fumbled to speak.

"Well. Usually, people around here know to turn their back to the wind and leaves. Well sometimes." he explained.

"Interesting." Elsa noted. "But yes. I just got here today."

"Well, welcome to Steeple Hills. I'm Jack." The boy smiled but didn't show his teeth.

"Elsa." She said.

"Well, it's been a pleasure meeting you, Elsa. Again, Welcome to Steeple Hills. Oh, and Happy Halloween." he said, walking away.

"Yeah. Same to you." Elsa said, though she wasn't sure if Jack heard her. She didn't understand it, but there was something about Jack that she found interesting.

"Who you talking to honey?" Wendy said, appearing as if out of thin air.

"Huh? Oh, just some guy. Welcomed us to town." Elsa said. It took her a second to realize Wendy wasn't alone. A man in a dark blue business suit stood next to her. His curly brown hair and his sparking brown eyes accompanied a teeth-baring smile.

"This is Mayor Stine." Wendy said. He held out his hand, but Elsa didn't shake it. He quickly retracted it. "Mr. Mayor this is my daughter -,"

"Elsa." She interrupted, trying to prevent her mother from calling her Ellie again.

"Well Elsa. It's a pleasure to meet you. Hopefully, you'll come to be right at home here in our little town."

The banner hanging above the street suddenly ripped in half, its bottom half descending onto the windshield of an oncoming car. The car stopped short, nearly causing an accident with the car behind it. "Dear God." Mayor Stine said. The people in the cars got out and looked at the other half of the banner. It was a perfect rip, right through the middle. Mayor Stine looked at Wendy and Elsa. "Please excuse me. Welcome to Steeple Hills Elsa. Wendy, welcome home." Mayor Stine ran to the scene. "Is everyone alright?"

"And there goes our first impression." Elsa quipped. "Yours at least." Wendy retorted. "Come on. Off to Spellman Drive."

"Last chance to turn around mom." Elsa said, wanting Wendy to go back to the city. Wendy shot her a look and Elsa knew what it meant. Elsa rolled her eyes as she got back in the car. Wendy got back into the car and drove off. Jack watched from the side of town hall, somewhat cowering behind the corner. As the car drove away, Jack pulled back, hiding himself from sight.

"Well. That's a first."

✳✳✳

The ride to Spellman Drive was quiet. The radio was turned down and Elsa's phone had died, her charger was packed up and out of her reach. Her headphones now resided in her jacket pocket. Wendy drove up a small hill past lines of trees on either side of the road; their half-naked branches formed an archway over Spellman Drive—a tunnel of gnarled limbs.

The house was the third house down on the left side of the street, once belonging to Wendy's parents. Elsa had last seen them when she was nine years old, and they visited her old home in the city for Christmas. They always showed Elsa pictures of Steeple Hills, calling it a beautiful place where ghouls loved to play, and planned to finally for her to visit.

Unfortunately, they ended up passing away within months of each other when Elsa was 13, before she could visit.

"This is the house?" Elsa asked.

"It sure is. Better looking in person." Wendy said as she parked in the driveway. Once she stepped out of the car, Elsa realized that the house looked the same as it did in the last picture her grandparents showed her of it: a small home of wood and brick with a large front porch.

"And you're positive there's no one else they could've left this house to? Like a brother or sister, that you never told me about?" Elsa asked.

"You know full well I was their only child." Wendy retorted.

Three rocking chairs close to the front window. Two of them were blue and green, but the small pink chair in between them looked worn; some of the paint had chipped away, revealing the dark and rotting wood underneath.

The roof looked to be missing a few tiles, but that didn't take away from the coziness the house's exterior expressed. The front door was white with a few chips in the paint. The rusty blue mailbox was losing more paint chips than the front door; the mailbox that bore the Walker family insignia had lost the letters L & R, now it read Wake. But even the K was beginning to peel off. The number on the mailbox was 31.

The front windows were decorated with cobwebs, Elsa could see they weren't the decoration kind. Remnants of torn Halloween decorations clung to pieces of tape along the gutters, some hung from staples hidden by the cobwebs on the windows. The front lawn was dying, and two dead trees resided by the porch. Well leafless trees at least. Several bigger trees cast a shadow over the house from the backyard. The driveway's black coating was partly cracked, and a bit raised, a tree stump resided on the right side of the driveway, the clear culprit of the cracking.

Elsa felt a chill in the air as she entered the house. She was slightly surprised as to how much bigger it looked on the inside. The walls were painted red, but years of sunlight had caused them to fade. The main staircase stopped at the entryway between the foyer and the kitchen. Some of the steps looked like they were ready to collapse. Elsa took a look into the kitchen, seeing the chair legs were lined with webs, cabinets and the table were practically painted with dust.
Wendy looked around the living room. "Wow. They never changed a thing in here." She noted.

The living room's white wallpaper was peeling at the corners, revealing a pink-ish coating underneath. The fireplace was black from old smoke use, the couch's brown cloth was as dusty as the kitchen table. The television had a combination of webs and dust on it. An old television, that still had the box on the back, took up space in the corner. The brand name looked like someone had taken it off with a screwdriver.
"I guess dusting wasn't an option." Elsa cracked. "Says the girl who never cleaned her bedroom." Wendy shot back.

All around the house, Elsa could see the sun blurred outline of frames, the nail holes were hard to miss. "Wow." Elsa said, amazed that her grandparents lived there. "If you think this is good, wait until you see your room." Wendy said, ignoring the sarcasm. "Oh joy." Wendy shot Elsa a look, though Elsa ignored it. She cautiously walked up the staircase. The steps creaked under her feet. "Guess Dad never got around to fixing that." Wendy said. "What was your first indication?" Elsa mumbled. Wendy heard that and didn't look happy.

The hallway at the top of the stairs was unusually humid, like someone had captured summer humidity in a jar and let it escape into the hall. Elsa walked down the old dirty beige carpeted hallway. She passed a door on her left; it was missing a doorknob; Elsa peeked inside seeing it was an empty room. A door on her right with the bottom half of the paint missing was cracked open, she peered inside seeing it was a bathroom. But it was the door at the end of the hall that caught her attention.

It was the only door that didn't have any deformity. The white paint looked fresh; the doorknob looked old, but intact at least. The knob had a small post-it note attached. The note read….

Elsa's Room

The writing on the note looked faded, further inspection showed that the post-it note was held to the doorknob by clear scotch tape. It clearly had been waiting there a while for Elsa. Elsa opened the door, seeing five steps with a wooden banister at the top. Reaching the top, Elsa looked around the room. It wasn't small or overly large, it felt more like a big living room. The floor had a gray-ish carpet that spanned the length of the room, also covering the wood floor underneath. Walls on both sides of the banister and around the room had paneling that looked brand new. By the banister lied four boxes stacked two and two, each marked Halloween with a taped piece of paper that read,

Whoever reads this, Please Don't throw away!

A post-it note stuck on the wall to Elsa's right.

It read; Couch goes here.

A second post-it note right next to it read;

Or here!

On the right side of the banister lied a small door. Elsa opened it up, a ball chain hung down. Pulling it turned on the dim lightbulb. In the dim light, Elsa could see a silver bar and a black shelf above it. This was definitely meant to be her closet. Two small windows resided on the left side of the room. They were covered in webbing. While the room looked great, something else caught Elsa's eye. A pair of aged orange curtains. She pulled them open the curtains with such, albeit unintended, force that it let some dust fall. Elsa had to cough out some dust that landed in her mouth. What lied behind the curtains was a round clear window.

Elsa couldn't take her eyes off it. Wendy appeared in the room at the top of the steps. "Wow. I didn't know they cleared out the attic." she said, admiring the emptiness of the room. "I've never seen it so empty. I remember when I couldn't walk up here without hitting something." Wendy said. She long wondered if her parents were hoarders. "Yeah." Elsa said, her attention still focused on the window. "AW. Mom and Dad's Halloween decorations. These were always fun. We should put these up." "Yeah sure. Sounds like a blast." Elsa said, coming to her senses. She laid the sarcasm on mud thick. "Watch it." Wendy looked at her. "Sorry." She said, sounding as insincere as she could. "Anyway, you sure you want this as your bedroom. My old bedroom is right downstairs." Wendy asked. "This will do." Elsa said.

Wendy could tell Elsa was trying to contain her excitement. "Ok. The delivery van just pulled up; your things will be up shortly." Wendy said.

✳✳✳

Later that night, Elsa lied awake in her twin sized bed, unable to sleep. Boxes marked ELLIE were spread across the floor. Only two of them were open. They were also crossed off and re-marked ELSA. She had opened the two smaller windows on the other side of the room to allow for some air, though she neglected to remove the webs first, it was surprisingly stuffy in there at night. She sat up in bed, soon sitting on the edge.

Elsa got up and walked over to the round window, feeling herself drawn to it. She, gently, opened the curtains. She didn't turn on any lights nor did she need to. The clear moonlight shined in through the window. It brightened up the room to the point of nearly blinding Elsa as she got closer to the window's glass. Looking out the window, Elsa was given a near crystal clear view of the trees and her neighbor's back yard. However, the large trees behind the houses seemed to move apart with the wind, appearing to form some sort of tunnel-like view that allowed Elsa to see over her neighbor's houses and see directly into Main Street. She didn't question it; she was too tired and a bit cranky from not being able to sleep to do so.

The Halloween decorations were in clear view. They lit up along with the lampposts, some blew and whistled with the occasional wind. Main Street looked peacefully beautiful at night. The hanging pumpkins swinging like pendulums with the wind. However, what caught Elsa's eye wasn't the bright lampposts or the trees with the swinging wake of streamers, but the person strolling by them. Jack seemed to be enjoying the silence of the night, no car, or another person in sight.

He kept his hood up as he strolled down the street with a smile on his face. He appeared to dig through piles of leaves before throwing or kicking them into the air with a childlike enjoyment of it. He kicked up a large pile of leaves by a lamppost, sending them into the air above him. He held out his arms and seemed to be dancing in the falling leaves like Kim in the falling ice in *Edward Scissorhands*, retaining a large smile on his face. Elsa couldn't understand it, she hated the move, and she wasn't thrilled about the town's first impression on her, but there was something about Jack that she found rather…. intriguing.

2
Restless

Elsa awoke the next morning to the sunlight shining in her eyes, she hadn't closed the round window's curtains before she fell asleep. She stood up, feeling the cold floor beneath her bare feet. She cracked her knuckles, then her neck. It was her morning routine.

She walked downstairs and through the hallway. It wasn't as humid in the morning. She cautiously walked down the main staircase. One or two steps creaked when she stepped on them. Walking into the kitchen, Elsa saw Wendy sitting at the kitchen table, it looked freshly cleaned. She was drinking coffee out of pumpkin shaped coffee mug which was a birthday present from her father. Wendy had woken up at six and had taken the time to clean up the kitchen and unpack every box meant for the room, Elsa saw the folded-up cardboard by the front door, looking like a stack of newspapers.

"Well good morning. Thought you were gonna try and sleep in on your first day of school." Wendy said. "Yeah well, the sun had other ideas." Elsa said, ignoring the school comment. She wasn't a morning person. "How did you sleep?" Wendy asked. "Eh." Elsa stated. Wendy took a swig of her coffee. "So," Wendy said, standing up. "Are you ready for your first day at school?" "Don't really have a choice now do I?" Elsa asked sarcastically as she made herself a bowl of cereal. "Still have a lot to unpack." "I'm sorry kiddo. The drive took longer than it should have. You can finish unpacking after school, or I could do it for you." Elsa shot Wendy a look and Wendy knew exactly what it meant. "Relax I'm kidding. Besides, I know it's gonna be tough starting a new school a month into the new term but, I have this feeling that you'll do fine Ellie."

"Elsa!" She again corrected Wendy. "Sorry." Elsa chowed down on the cereal, quickly finishing it.
The cuckoo clock hanging above the kitchen entry way sounded at the change of the hour.

"It's time. It's time. You're gonna be late."
A small raven emerged from the top of the clock, then quickly retreated inside when it was done. Elsa looked at the clock, then back at her mother. Wendy knew why. "Yeah, that clock's getting moved." She said. "How about just taking it down." Elsa said coldly. "Believe it or not, it used to be much worse." "Oh, I believe it." Elsa said as she walked away. "Remember school starts in forty." Wendy called. Elsa walked up the stairs, she tripped over one of the steps going up. "OW." She said. "You alright?" Wendy ran into the foyer. "Just fine." Elsa said, a bit frustrated. "That's it. I'm getting those stairs fixed." Wendy said. "Like that'll help." Elsa mumbled as she stood up and returned upstairs.

✳✳✳

Elsa was back downstairs in twenty minutes. She put her dirty white sneakers back on, along with a new pair of jeans that were ripped at the right knee and a black t-shirt that simply read, in orange lettering …BOO.

This shirt was equipped with Elsa's black leather jacket and her sunglasses, that were now covering her eyes. Wendy got one look at the outfit. "Do you have any outfits without the jacket and glasses?" She asked, throwing in some sarcasm. Elsa nodded. "Didn't think so."

Wendy said for she didn't want to have the argument and make Elsa late. Though she really knew Elsa would fight her tooth and nail on it. "Come on." Wendy handed Elsa a dark red backpack, "You're well prepared. Two notebooks and a few pens are inside."

"Seriously?" Elsa asked. "Just take the bag. You'll do fine at Gillman." Wendy said as they walked out the door.

3
The Eeriness

The local high school, Gillman High, was a nice sized building. A tall brick and cement building with a wide front entrance and a wider courtyard off to the side, residing on Chaney Pl. The flagpole had a big orange and black pumpkin shaped flag flying beneath the American flag. Elsa reluctantly walked into the school.

The school's interior looked nice, beige metal lockers that had a few dents, Halloween posters covering most of the white plaster walls, along with some framed corkboards. Very few lockers had their exteriors customized, most students preferred to decorate the interior instead. All the students kept sneaking quick glances at Elsa like she had a disease. Elsa was never the one to pay attention to peer pressure, never caring what others thought of her.
She rounded the corner, not bothering to figure out which locker was her. She found the main office with ease. She walked inside, feeling a rush of cold air hit her. She wasn't sure if there was a window open or if someone still had their air conditioning on in October.

The secretary, Mrs. Strode, sat at her desk, her blonde hair tied in a bun. She kept her hazel eyes covered by thick framed glasses, but the curl in her lip was hard to ignore. She stared at her computer screen. Even through her sunglasses, Elsa could see the reflection of cat videos on YouTube in Mrs. Strode's glasses. "What do you need?" Mrs. Strode asked. Her voice was low almost like a whisper.
"New student. Elsa Carlyle. Apparently I need a schedule." Mrs. Strode never took her eyes off the computer as she reached for a purple folder under her computer.

"Welcome to Gillman, new girl." The way Mrs. Strode spoke; it was almost as if helping Elsa came at the most inconvenient time.

"Did I hear someone say new student?" A tall man with pale skin approached slowly. He wore a black suit with a light blue tie, against a bright green shirt. "I'm guessing you must be Elsa Carlyle." His voice was a bit gravelly. "Excuse my voice, I made the mistake of chugging my hot coffee this morning." He coughed hard as if to clear his throat. He failed to see that Elsa didn't care.

"Anyway, it is rather strange getting a new student this late into the school year, but, nonetheless. Welcome. I'm Vice Principal Myers. If you ever need anything, do consider coming to me." He shifted his gaze to the clock that hung above the door, then quickly looked back at Elsa. "Oh, it looks like class is about to start." Mrs. Strode let out a sigh of annoyance as she held out Elsa's schedule. "Looks like you need to go to room one hundred and three. Better move quick. Bell will be ringing soon. Have a good day." Myers handed Elsa the paper, smiled, then walked back the way he came. Elsa stuffed the paper into her bag and walked out of the office.

"I already hate this." She said to herself.

✳✳✳

She walked into the small classroom marked 103. Two large windows were on the left side of the room, the curtains were pulled open, and the blinds look glued to the top of the windows, 15 desks occupied the middle of the room. Elsa took a seat near the door as the bell rang. She ignored the possible eardrum damage. One of the windows was left cracked open to allow the brisk autumn breeze to creep into the room. A few leaves accompanied the breeze through the slightly ripped screen.

Several more students crammed into the room as the teacher, Ms. Astra Shelley, walked in. "Good morning class." She said, with some pep in her voice. Ms. Shelley looked like your run of the mill English teacher. Dressed in a white button-down blouse with long brown kakis that ran down to her black sneakers. The only thing that differentiated her from any other English teacher was the streak of orange in her brown, and graying, hair, and the yellow tinge in her right eye. "Now class, I've been told we have a new student. Please welcome..." Ms. Shelley had to squint through her thick framed glasses to see the name on her computer, she hated her computer. "Ellie Carlyle. Stand up Ellie." Elsa reluctantly stood up now even angrier at Wendy. She hated it when teachers did something like this, because above all of the things she hated, she hated being the center of attention the most.
"Class say hello."

"Hello." The students said in unison, though it sounded half-hearted.

"For future reference. My name is Elsa." Elsa said coldly, then sat back down. Ms. Shelley didn't know how to respond other than "Oh. Ok." She quickly fixed the name on her computer. "Now class, last week we discussed starting Shakespeare. But I've made a decision. Halloween is right around the corner, so I thought it would be fun to take a break from our regular English lit to do something a little bit more," Ms. Shelley shrugged her shoulders. "Bone chilling." She added, shaking her shoulders to make her point. Elsa tilted her head back, beginning to slouch in her seat.

The class sighed in relief in delaying the start of reading Shakespeare. "Instead, I have a small project for you all." Ms. Shelley explained, which caused a semi-united groan from the class. "Now. Now. Hear me out. I want you all to read any scary book you can get your hands on. It can be *Goosebumps*," One hand shot up, interrupting Ms. Shelley. "ONLY the books Robert!" Ms. Shelley put emphasis on the word only. The hand lowered. "In addition, you may also read *Fear Street* or *Scary Stories to tell in the dark* or whatever scary stories you feel inspired by." Several students seemed pleased with the material provided. "I want you all to write your own Halloween story. Now, I want this to be a group project, but no more than two people. Most importantly, be original. If I detect any ounce of plagiarism that's more than a sentence you will pay for it dearly. I want them on my desk by the end of class on Halloween. I want you all to have fun with it. Just not too much fun, keep it clean please." Ms. Shelley peered down to the back of the room. "Monica."

In the back was a young woman with dirty blonde hair that was tied in a ponytail. She had her head in her notebook, sketching the head of the Frankenstein monster along with old fashions ghosts. There were smaller doodles of tombstones and coffins along the edges of the paper. She didn't seem to be paying attention.

"Monica!" Ms. Shelley raised her voice. Monica's head shot up. "Huh?" She asked. "I was saying that for a project, I want you all to write your own Halloween story. Have fun with it, but please keep it clean." Ms. Shelley clarified. "Define clean." Monica quipped. "No blood, no guts, no gore." Ms. Shelley practically ordered in a rapid-fire dialect, like Hades from *Hercules*. "So, no Werewolves, Vampires, or even one angry ghost?" Monica sarcastically asked. Ms. Shelley didn't look amused. "Monica. Please. Keep your story clean, if you want to involve those creatures go ahead. But none of what I mentioned."

"Then there's no point. Vampires drink blood, Werewolves cause gore, and even Frankenstein is made from dead body parts." Monica argued. Several students groaned.

One male student groaned, "The freak is at it again."

"All I'm saying is, by making those rules, you're killing my creativity." Monica argued.

"Who cares?" The same male student complained. "Your stories suck anyway. All they do is confuse and make people sick. I mean seriously Monica go to a head doctor or something, get that monster mania sense of yours checked," The student continued.

"Hunter!" Ms. Shelley called, slamming a book on her desk. Hunter fell silent. "Monica. Write whatever you want. But I don't want ten pages of blood and definitely no dream stalking or possessed toys." Ms. Shelley ordered. "Sure." Monica said sadly. "Anyway, the library received a stockpile of *Goosebumps* yesterday, so be sure to take advantage of that for your story. Any questions?" Ms. Shelley asked.

✷✷✷

At the end of the school day, Monica walked outside. Her backpack hanging from her right shoulder, slightly torn open just under the zipper.

"Hey freak." Hunter came practically sprinting after her.

"Not now Hunter."

"Oh, now seems perfect." Hunter jumped in front of Monica, blocking her path. An arrogant smile on his face. Monica couldn't ignore

21

the pimples forming under his nose, "So, Whatcha gonna write about huh? Vampire ballerinas? Rotting corpses hidden in trees?" Hunter mocked. "How about the most horrifying thing of all. You thinking you'll ever have friends." Hunter's smiling expression faded into a scowl. "Look Hunter just,"

"Just what? What are you gonna do?" Hunter didn't give Monica time to answer as he swatted her backpack right off her shoulder, sending her notebooks flying out across the schoolyard. Several students laughed as Monica tripped trying to pick up her books. They chanted freak in a mocking fashion, some even calling her Monster Monica. "You hear that?" Hunter asked, squatting down to be face to face with Monica. "Looks like people do know your name." He mocked.

Two boys stood by the school's entrance. One took a step forward, "I'm not taking another," "Hold up cuz. Look." What the boy was referring to was how in his mocking and humiliating of Monica, Hunter didn't see someone approach him from behind nor hear the crowd go silent. But he sure felt the tug on the back of his collar. The tug pulled the front of the shirt into Hunter's throat, slightly choking him as he was pulled backwards and down, his head hitting the ground. He looked up, seeing Elsa standing over him.

"Leave. Her. Alone." Elsa coldly demanded. Hunter struggled to his feet.

He met Elsa face to face, albeit by an inch or two. "Stay out of this newbie." Hunter ordered. "Make me." Elsa challenged. Even though her sunglasses, she stared deep into Hunter's eyes. A hint of bloodshot in his blue eyes. Hunter stepped closer. "You wanna try that again?" Elsa could smell what Hunter had for lunch on his breath, while it fogged up her glasses.

"Get, your garbage breath off my glasses." Elsa coldly stated, pushing Hunter out of her face. The surrounding students let a loud OOOOOOOO in unison.

Hunter wiped the little dirt that was on his shirt. "Look at that everyone. Monster Monica has her first friend. Eerie Elsa!" He started to laugh and walked away, failing to notice he was the only one laughing. Elsa walked over to Monica, who had cleaned up her notebooks. She pulled Monica to her feet.

"Thank you." She whispered to Elsa, the hint of tears in her eyes. Elsa made sure Monica had everything in order before Monica walked away. Elsa walked away in the other direction. She passed the two boys on her way off the school grounds, not bothering to look at them. The two boys looked at each other, "Best not to mess with her." "Agreed." The boy's cousin agreed with a sly smile.

4

William Shakespook

Elsa walked down Main Street, taking in the visuals of the town she was now forced to live in. While she wasn't fully aware of the town or its streets, she chose to walk in order walk off her frustration. She didn't care that she didn't know her way home, subconsciously hoping she would find some magical shortcut back to NYC. She walked past piles of leaves that seem to cling to the lampposts, some piles looked raked, cleaning up Jack's nighttime handiwork. She stopped in front of Poe's Pet shop. She looked in the window, seeing the inside decorations replicated Main Street's decorations.

Orange and black streamers hung from the lights. Small little ghost lights hung from the shelves. A small wolf cub jumped in Elsa's view; it resided alone in the window. Elsa looked down at the cub, taking off her sunglasses. It had black fur with a white ring around its left eye. It seemed to wave at Elsa with its paw. Elsa knelt down, getting to the cub's eye level. He approached the window, keeping his cute eyes locked on Elsa. She smiled, albeit briefly, the cub squished its nose against the glass. Elsa couldn't help but fall victim to the cuteness of the cub.

She stood up, flashing a friendly smirk to the cub, which the little cub responded with a wave. As she put her sunglasses back on, Elsa got a look inside. Mr. Poe, at least that's who she thought it was, stood at the register, wearing a red sweater that looked like it once belonged to Mr. Rogers.

He stood at about 6 feet tall, some gray hair ran from ear to ear behind his head and stopped at his neck, just missed the top of his head, his eyes covered by a pair of thin glasses with scotch tape wrapped around the center. If there was one thing the window didn't cover up, it was that Mr. Poe's left arm was nonexistent. Mr. Poe looked at Elsa, baring a smile that showed off his yellow teeth, he waved in a friendly manner with his right arm, she awkwardly nodded her head before walking away.

As Elsa continued on, she looked at the busy street, the vintage cars catching her eye. Being in NYC the majority of her life, Elsa was used to seeing Taxi Cabs and buses, but never regular cars.

The swift yet brisk fall breeze blew through, the orange and black streamers swayed with it, as did the small lights and lamppost pumpkins. A few of the small pumpkins had their tops chewed up.

Despite all the people passing her on the street, Elsa couldn't help but get the feeling someone was following her. She kept turning her head every ten steps or so but saw no one coming in her direction. She wondered if Hunter was trying to get some payback. Elsa never backed down from a fight, she was more than ready for Hunter to try something.

When she turned her head forward, after the seventh look back, she saw the town bus roll away from the bus stop. It wasn't one of those big plastic shelters with a metal bench inside, but rather an old-style wooden bench out in the open. On that bench sat Jack, he looked like he had been sitting there a while. He still wore the gray hoodie and long blue jeans, though his sneakers looked a little bit dirtier. His hood was covering his head again. He sat on the bench, just looking from left to right like he was waiting for someone to arrive, his hands tapping on his knees.

"Hey!" Elsa called as she approached the bench. Jack didn't move, continuing to tap his knees.

"Hey!" Elsa called again. Jack moved his head to the left, catching Elsa in the corner of his eye. She sarcastically waved her hand, "Hey you!" He looked to the right then back to Elsa.

"Me?" He pointed to himself.

"No, the old lady sitting next to you, yes you." Elsa confirmed sarcastically.

"Interesting. Guess the first time wasn't a fluke." He mumbled to himself.

"What?" Elsa asked.

"Oh nothing. Elsa, right?" Jack asked.

"Yeah, and you're Jack." Elsa confirmed, the sarcasm hadn't faded. Jack smiled, but still didn't show his teeth.

"You remembered." He said, appearing a bit surprised, but also a bit touched.

"Remembered what? Your name?" Elsa asked, her sarcasm faded.

"Yeah. A lot of people tend to forget it." Jack explained. Elsa didn't know what to make of that, except to start feeling sorry for Jack.

"Uh huh." She said, leaning against the bench.

"Guess you got a good memory." Jack said.

"Looks like you do too." Elsa pointed out.

"Not that good." Jack argued.

"You remembered my name." Elsa retorted.

"I tend to remember a lot of things that stick out to me. A name like Elsa definitely sticks out. No offense." Jack explained.

"None taken." Elsa said, though she rolled her eyes under her glasses.

"I'm weird like that." Jack said. This got a slight laugh out of Elsa. "If you don't mind me asking. What's your last name?" Jack asked.

"Carlyle." Elsa said. "You?"

"Harvey." Jack said.

"Well Jack Harvey, it looks like you missed your bus." Elsa joked.

"Oh, actually I was just sitting here. I wasn't really expecting the bus. I just felt like sitting down." Jack said.

"HHMPH." Elsa expressed, she didn't understand why, but Jack was becoming more intriguing to her. His quirkiness was something she had never seen before, well not at Jack's level.

"Yeah, when you walk around town all day. You get the urge to sit down every once in a while. Just take a load off." Jack added as he stretched his legs.

"That makes sense." Elsa said.

"Now it's time for me to start walking again." Jack said as he stood up.

"You're welcome to join me." He added. Elsa thought about it.

"Yeah, why not."

"If you want. I can show you some of the shortcuts around town." Jack suggested.

"Shortcuts?" Elsa asked.

"Oh yeah. I know a bunch of them."

"Sure." Elsa said. "Gonna need some in case I ever want to leave this town."

"Nice shirt by the way." Jack complimented, trying to ignore the comment. Elsa looked at her shirt then back at Jack.

"Thanks." Elsa said. "You always wear that hoodie?" Elsa bluntly asked.

"Not always. Only in Fall and Winter." Jack said with a smile.

"Do you always keep the hood up?" Elsa asked.

"Only when I wear the hoodie." Jack retorted.

The two walked down Main Street, passing various shops that had people in and out the front doors every few minutes. Jack waved at a few, but they kept walking. One woman walked out of Stoker's groceries, carrying a bag of apples. "Hey Ms. Ross." Jack said. But Ms. Ross kept walking. Elsa found that rude, she looked back at Ms. Ross.

"Don't worry about it. Ms. Ross ignores everyone. She's a miserable old woman." Jack explained.

"Still." Jack just shrugged his shoulders.

"I'm used to it." Jack looked at a few piles of leaves.

"Guess you didn't get to kick those last night." Elsa quipped. Jack looked at her and started laughing.

"You saw that?" Elsa nodded. "Please don't tell anyone it's me doing it. No fun if they know." Jack smiled.

"Sure whatever." Elsa said. "Why do you do it anyway?" She asked.

"Sometimes I just like to walk through town at night, I enjoy the peace and quiet. No hundreds of cars honking all night. I mean the bus rolls through, but that's nothing, helps me clear my head. Plus kicking the leaves is just too much fun to pass up, especially at night." Jack explained.

"Ok. So how does that explain you holding your arms out while they fall?" Elsa asked. Jack's eyes shot open.

"You saw that too?" Elsa nodded. "Now I'm really embarrassed." He
said. Elsa smirked. "Just for fun." He added. Jack didn't have any other
answer than that. His childlike enjoyment peaked Elsa's interest further.

"Interesting." She said. That's when Elsa caught sight of the new
banner for the Halloween Festival. "So. What can you tell me about this
Halloween festival?" Elsa asked, changing the subject.

"Oh. Well, that. It usually starts soon after the sun sets. They bring out
all the pumpkin food and drinks,"

"Pumpkin food and drinks?" Elsa asked.
"Oh yeah. This town goes nuts around pumpkin season. Almost
everything is pumpkin. Pie, whipped cream, any kind of cookie, donuts,
milkshakes, even the hot chocolate." Jack explained.

"Wait, pumpkin hot chocolate?" Elsa asked.
"Yeah. It's pretty good, goes well with the pumpkin cream cookies and
donuts over at Mel's diner. It's a lot better than the pumpkin coffee."
Jack said, shuttering a bit at the memory of the pumpkin coffee.

"Huh." Elsa said.
"Then once the sun has set and it's completely dark in the sky, they shut
off all the lights inside the buildings and let the decorations light up
Main Street. There's a small parade with the firemen and police." Jack
explained.

"CAW!"

The cawing of the crow stole their attention. Elsa looked around
and saw that she and Jack had stopped in front of the cemetery.
"Whoa." She said. Through the view from the Iron Gate, which read
Whipstaff Cemetery, the place looked to go on for a few miles.

29

"Yeah. The cemetery is huge. Some people go in there because it's quiet and kind of a good place to get a walk in. Not so bad." Jack said. Elsa suddenly felt a chill down her spine, she looked over to Jack. He had this sad look on his face while gazing at the cemetery.

"You, ok?" Elsa asked, mentally wondering why she asked.

"Yeah. Yeah. I just have someone close in there." He said.

"Oh." Elsa said, feeling a bit awkward.

"It's ok. You know maybe we should get you home." Jack began to walk away. Elsa could sense Jack's sadness. But felt he wasn't telling her everything. When she looked back at the cemetery, she noticed the few people she saw appeared to have this blueish tint to them. Elsa started to wonder if she was wearing her sunglasses for too long.

"Hey um," Jack broke Elsa's staring. "I just realized I have no clue where you live." Jack said with a smile.

"Right. I think, what was it called? Oh, Spellman." Elsa said. Jacks smiled dropped.

"Spellman Drive?"

"Yeah." Elsa confirmed. "Why?" She asked.

"No reason. Just never knew anyone who lived on that street. But I know where that is." Jack explained. Elsa's eyebrow rose up.

"You know Jack. You're kinda weird."

"Not the first time I've heard that." Jack said.

"But you're not so bad." Elsa said.

"Definitely the first time I've heard that." Jack smiled. Jack took another look at the cemetery, getting a view of the two crypts near the back.

"Come on. Maybe you can show me a shortcut."

"Oh no problem there." Jack said walking ahead of Elsa.

As the two walked away, something watched them from behind the crypts. Letting out a grunt like moan as Jack and Elsa turned a corner.

"Harvey!"

5

Things Out There

Jack and Elsa headed up Spellman Dr. Elsa's new house wasn't hard to find, for Elsa at least. Approaching the house, Jack stopped in his tracks. He jerked his head backwards, confusingly staring into the distance. Elsa turned towards him.

"You, ok?" She asked.

"Yeah. Um, did you hear that?" Jack asked.

"Hear what?" Elsa asked.

"I guess not. I think I'm hearing things." Jack said, tugging on his right ear. Elsa didn't know what to make of that, she didn't feel completely awkward, but she was getting close to it.

"Anyway, thanks for showing me the shortcut. Didn't think it be easy to get to Spellman from Whipstaff."

"Well, when you walk around town as much as I do, you tend to discover new ways to get around faster." Jack quipped.

"Oh, I don't think anyone walks around town as much as you Jack." Elsa said.

"Probably not." Jack smiled. "So, I'll see you around?" He said, though he sounded like he was asking.

"Yeah, see you around." Elsa walked up the driveway, Jack watched as she walked inside. She waved at Jack one last time before closing the door. Jack turned and walked away.

"This is quite interesting." He said to himself.

Wendy sat in the living room, she struggled to get a good picture on the old television. She noticed Elsa tossing her bag into the kitchen. "Hey kiddo." Elsa noticed the stairs looked different, instead of the almost breaking under pressure staircase the stairs looked newly built, even the railing looked new. "What happened to the stairs?" She asked, taking off her sunglasses. Wendy got up from the couch, defeated by the television, entering the foyer to look at the stairs. "You know, I forgot how fast you can get things fixed in this town. The guys were here at nine and gone by two. Amazing work, right?" Elsa knew what Wendy was trying to do.

"I know you're trying to push the small-town living." Elsa observed, she tried her best not to sound obnoxious. "Is it that obvious?" Wendy asked sarcastically. Elsa jokingly sighed. "So how was school?" Wendy asked. "School is school. Nothing different than in New York. Though the professors don't assign projects on your first day." Elsa said coldly. "Even when your first day is near the end of October?" Wendy asked, crossing her arms, and arching her eyebrow. Elsa realized Wendy had outwitted her, though Elsa realized too late she set herself up for it. "I got assigned a writing project due on Halloween." Elsa explained. "Really? Which teacher?" Wendy asked. "Ms. Shelley. I think. I can't remember." Elsa didn't want to remember. She held out a little hope Wendy would take her back to NYC and put her back in school there.

"Ms. Shelley?" Wendy asked, surprised. "Wait. Astra Shelley?" Elsa looked at her mother. "I'm guessing you had her mom?" Elsa sarcastically asked.

"I did. Honestly thought she would've retired by now." Wendy said. "But what about this project?" Wendy asked, walking into the kitchen. "Just a small scary story. Ms. Shelley says it's for fun." Elsa explained, though Wendy could tell she didn't really wanna talk. "For fun? Sounds like Ms. Shelley has changed since I had her. Back then she was stricter than a prison warden." Wendy explained.

"The rest of the teachers sure felt like that. Math with Mr. Stoker was just horrendous. Science with Ms. Krueger was just her repeating the same formula on the board like twenty times. History with Mr. Hodder was by far the worst, he kept mumbling and what he put on the board was just chicken scratch." Elsa explained.
"Now that sounds like the teachers I had. Consider yourself lucky with Ms. Shelley. Closest thing to fun my teachers did was humming Christmas carols in December, and I still think that was required by the principal." Wendy said. "Why required?" Elsa asked.
"Honestly, I think the principal wanted them to have a little spirit. Especially around the holidays. Your grandfather got a kick out of it." Wendy explained. Elsa arched her eyebrow, finally taking off her glasses.

"So, did you meet any new people?" Wendy asked. "Not particularly. Then again, I wasn't looking." Elsa said. Wendy sighed softly. She was beginning to get frustrated with Elsa's attitude. "That's good. I'm gonna get started on dinner, you go get started on the mountain of homework you have." Wendy said. "How do you know I have a mountain of homework?" Elsa asked, trying to be slick. "You forget kiddo. I went to Gillman too and judging by the names you dropped, I had the exact same teachers you do." Wendy stated, a smirk on her face and her eyebrow raised. Elsa realized her mother had gotten the upper hand. She shook her head and grabbed her bag. Not saying a word, but keeping the smirk, Elsa walked upstairs.

✳✳✳

Elsa sat on her bed Indian style, her socks in contrast with each other. One was black, the other was white with a hint of a hole forming at the toes. She stared at the blank screen of the laptop that rested in front of her. Several unpacked boxes resided by the banister, while the decoration boxes now took up space in the hall. Elsa had to dig her laptop out of her suitcase, she had buried it in between her clothes. One of Elsa's boxes lay at the foot of her bed, its contents that of hardcover and paperback novels.

Elsa dug out five *Goosebumps* novels; their covers were clean, but the spines looked somewhat cracking. The five novels were *The Haunted Mask, Monster Blood, Ghost Beach, The Barking Ghost,* and *The Headless Ghost* were sprawled out around the bed behind Elsa. Copies of *Stephen King's The Shining* and *Pet Semetary* rested on top of the box.

The rest of her homework lay dormant in her bag on the floor. But yet, despite the books around her, Elsa couldn't help but think about Jack. She didn't understand why Jack was able to get inside her head, but his kindness and quirkiness seemed to get through Elsa's tough exterior and stick with her like gum to the bottom of a sneaker. Elsa was just finishing the page, when a sudden pinging on her phone diverted her attention. The phone was wedged under her left leg, she expected it to be the usual spam email, but instead saw a Facebook notification.

Elsa aimed her eyes at her laptop, switching tabs to the log in page. Elsa barely used her Facebook to begin with. Logging onto the page, Elsa could see she had only one notification. It was a simple friend request; it was the first friend request Elsa had received in a while. The list of friends on her account stopped at ten, mainly people she went to school with, but she didn't consider them real friends.

Clicking the request, Elsa expected an account of someone who shared mutual friends with her but didn't actually know Elsa. Instead, she saw a request from someone she recognized, well sort of, the name read…. Monica King.

Elsa clicked on Monica's account, finding numerous monster pictures and links to a website of short stories. Monica's profile picture was the only one picture of her on her account. It was of a selfie of Monica standing in front of a mirror, staring at the mirror as if she was staring into space.

Monica's friends list was lower than Elsa's. Most of the comments on Monica's pictures were rather mean and repetitive, the most common one was calling her the Mortician and Freak. Monster Monica was the most recent comment slam posted. Elsa didn't click confirm or ignore. She left the friend request as it was and logged out of her account. "Ellie! Dinner!" Wendy called from downstairs. Elsa rolled her eyes, closing her laptop.

"And the name game continues." Elsa cracked. She got off her bed, quickly falling to the floor with a thud. Elsa didn't need to think twice to realize her feet had fallen asleep. "OW."

✳✳✳

"So, how's that project coming along?" Wendy asked, she sat across from Elsa at the table. Elsa couldn't speak, her mouth was full of rice. She held up her index finger, signaling to give her a minute. She

swallowed the lump of rice, a little pain in her throat. "Working on it."
She said. "How long does it have to be?" "No clue." Elsa clarified.
"Interesting. Never heard of Ms. Shelley not giving a page limit." Wendy
said.

"Guess she has changed since your day." Elsa said, putting a sarcastic
emphasis on HAS. "Sounds like it." Wendy noted, ignoring the sarcasm.
"Did Ms. Shelley give any rules regarding the project?" Wendy asked,
taking in a forkful of rice. "Just it has to be handed in on Halloween. Got
to keep it clean blah blah blah." Elsa stated. "Keep it clean?" Wendy
asked, some food still in her mouth.

"She singled out this one girl." "Yeah? Did you get a name?"
"Morgana, Morticia, Monica, something like that." Elsa said. While she
did remember Monica's name, she didn't want to give Wendy any idea
she bothered to pay attention to any other person in Steeple Hills. "Why
did she single her out?" "Something about this girl having a," "Over-
active imagination?" Wendy asked. "Exactly." "Well, judging from how
Ms. Shelley told her to keep it clean, I'm guessing this girl has a knack
for writing straight up gore." Wendy noted, taking in a fork full of
chicken.

"Guess so." Elsa said, taking in some tomatoes. "You know, if
you ended up working with this girl, you two could be quite the team.
Might scare Ms. Shelley." Wendy said, though the part about scaring
Ms. Shelley was meant to be sarcastic. Elsa smirked sarcastically, but the
thought of scaring a teacher did entertain her.

✳✳✳

Around midnight on Spellman Drive, the moon was bright in the sky, stars gathered near the moon like it was a school librarian telling kindergarteners a story. A brisk autumn night breeze blew through, shaking the trees, lightly painting the sidewalk and road with leaves. Jack Harvey walked up and down the street, finding no leave piles to kick. He looked up to the night sky, seeing the stars and the moon. He shrugged his shoulders, "Back to main street then." He said with slight optimism in his voice.

"Jack!" A female voice in the wind called to Jack. He turned around in various directions to see where it came from but saw nothing. "Jack Harvey!" He turned around again, but tripped over his own feet, stumbling backwards, and knocking over the trashcan. Jack looked down at the can, which looked like it threw up the garbage, and the scent wasn't any better.

"Oops." He said with a tinge of fear in his voice. He looked around the neighborhood, seeing all of the houses were pitch black. "Huh, I hope no one heard that." The interior and exterior lights of the house suddenly kicked on. Jack quickly looked, uttering in a cartoonish voice "Uh oh," before running off.

6
A Fond Memory

Elsa walked into Ms. Shelley's class, she kept a black Frankenstein t-shirt hidden under her leather jacket, her sunglasses still on. Monica sat at the back of the room just like yesterday, her hair tied in a ponytail. She sat there sketching a monstrous looking pumpkin in her notebook. Elsa sat at the desk parallel to Monica. Monica noticed and smiled at Elsa.

"Hey." She whispered. Elsa nodded her head as her reply. "Did you get the friend request?" Monica whispered.

"Haven't been on my Facebook lately." Elsa whispered.
"Oh." Monica said. She returned to sketching in her notebook.

"Hey." Monica looked at Elsa. "Can you do me a favor?" Elsa asked. Monica set down her pencil. "What's up?" Elsa leaned in.

"You've lived in this town your whole life, right?"
"Yeah." Monica confirmed.

"Since it's pretty much clear to me I'm staying here. You be the best one to give me the low down on the people here, right?" Monica let out a small laugh through her nose.
"Sure. Who do you want to start with?"

The two boys from the day before walked in. Both were brunette, one standing at six feet, the one behind him appeared slightly shorter. They both sat down, sitting one behind the other. Their desks were close to the window.

"Those two." Elsa whispered.
"That's Marcus and Finn Deetz. They live over on Roth Street." Monica whispered.

"Which one is which?" Elsa asked.

"The one in long sleeves and walks with a bit of a hunch is Finn." Monica explained. Elsa took notice. "To be honest, I think he walks with a hunch to differentiate himself from Marcus." Monica explained.

"Are they twins or something?" Elsa asked.

"Just cousins but are like brothers. Both born in the same year. Just three weeks apart." Monica explained. "Oh, don't bother asking Finn out?" She added.

"Why? Big heartbreaker?"

"Actually no. Girls always ask him out, but Finn," Monica paused for a bit. "Honestly, I think he's caught up in his own world."

"And Marcus, is it?" Elsa asked.

"Yeah. He's kind of the more vocal of the two, but he's not really one for hanging out much after school with anyone recently. Last few years he's just been here, work, and home. Nothing much else." Monica explained.

"HHMPH." Elsa said. Ms. Shelley walked in; Hunter followed. "One more thing." Monica whispered. "No matter who or what you are, if you mess with Finn, you mess with Marcus and vice versa." Monica explained.

"Good morning class. Hope you are all enjoying your project." Ms. Shelley rhetorically asked. The class uttered a collective groan. Ms. Shelley rolled her eyes, "I'm going to take that as a Yes Ms. Shelley." Ms. Shelley said sarcastically. "Anyway, who here would like to discuss their project?" Ms. Shelley asked. Monica raised her hand. "Ah Monica." Ms. Shelley said, though she didn't sound too happy Monica raised her hand. "What have you decided to write about?"

"Probably Zombie cheerleaders at war with Vampire football players." Hunter remarked. He had this arrogant smile on his face that went well with his arrogant laugh, only thing was that he was the only one laughing, again failing to notice it. He caught a glimpse of Elsa, his smile again fading into a scowl.

"Actually no. I'm writing about a…" "Hold on Monica." Ms. Shelley interrupted. "Does this story abide by the rules I gave you yesterday?" "Yes." Monica confirmed. "Carry on then."
"It's mainly a story about the old grounds by the cemetery." Monica briefly explained. "Interesting concept." Ms. Shelley said. "Why there?" She asked. "It's one of the spookiest places in Steeple Hills,"

"Are you kidding me?" Hunter looked back at Monica. "Can't you let that old fable go? It never happened. Let it go Monster Monica." Hunter said.
"Why don't you grow up?" Elsa asked, having enough of Hunter.

"Oh, look the newbie is standing up for the freak again. Just what we need a pair of freaks that," "HUNTER!" Ms. Shelley yelled. "Hallway now!" She demanded. "For what? I didn't do anything." Hunter complained.
"Except disrespect a tragedy," Marcus interjected. "And the memory of the victims of it." Finn interjected.

"I don't need play by play from the Deetz boys." Hunter said. "Yeah, well if you listened to any play by play maybe you wouldn't suck as quarterback." Marcus quipped. The class let out a collective "OOOOOOO!"
"You two wanna take this outside?" Hunter threatened.

"Hunter two on one isn't a fair fight. But I will gladly take you on mano a mano." Marcus challenged. "Marcus, he can't win a game with a team behind him, you think he's gonna win a fight on his own?" Finn asked sarcastically.

Elsa leaned towards Monica.

"Wow. You weren't kidding."

"Nope." Monica confirmed.

"Hunter. Hallway. Now!" Ms. Shelley demanded, finally having enough of Hunter's attitude. Hunter collected his bag and walked out into the hall, eyeing Monica, and Elsa as he walked out. "Monica I am," "Don't worry about it. Let's get on with class." Monica said with a smile. Elsa looked at Monica, even though she didn't know her well, she could tell Monica was hiding her real feelings behind the smile. Elsa knew that look all too well. "Now, Monica. Do you have a partner?" Ms. Shelley asked. Monica's eyes shot open, "Uhhhhhhh."

✳✳✳

Monica stood outside, leaning against a tree that still had brown leaves on it, though only on the top, and there were very few. The bottom of the tree was rather dead. Her backpack around her left shoulder, pinned between her side and the tree. She bit down on the nail of her left thumb; she already chewed her right thumb nail until she couldn't chew it anymore. Monica continued to bite on her nail, almost in a trance-like state, almost like she was trying to sharpen it. Hunter never returned to the classroom after he was kicked out. Monica felt her heart race as her anxiety overcame her, feeling Hunter would try to do something outside. She chewed her thumb nail until she hit the tip of her thumb, soon debating whether to move onto her index finger or not. She kept looking around for Hunter, her right hand unable to decide whether to become a fist or just take up space in the pocket of Monica's black pants.

Hunter emerged from the school; his eyes locked on Monica like a wolf to his prey. A cool breeze blew through as he approached Monica. She turned around quick to meet his gaze like she sensed his presence. In her pocket, Monica's right hand balled into a fist. Hunter stood there, not saying a word, but his arrogant smile visible.

"Well," That was until he felt a tap on his shoulder. He turned seeing Elsa, her sunglass covering her eyes. A sarcastic smile on her face.

"Do you really want to do this again?" She asked. Hunter looked back and forth between Elsa and Monica.

He sighed, shook his head, and uttered "Later freaks." Then walked away.

Elsa looked at Monica.

"You good?" She half-heartedly asked.

"Yeah. Thank you." Monica said.

"No problem." Elsa went to walk away.

"Hey wait." Monica called. Elsa stopped and looked back at her. "Ms. Shelley told me I need a partner."

"Didn't she say some people can work alone?" Elsa asked.

"She did. But after class she made it clear to me that I need a partner this time." Monica explained. Elsa had a feeling where this was going.

"She made us partners, didn't she?" Elsa asked, sounding a bit mad at it.

"Not exactly." Monica said. Elsa shook her head, her tongue pressing against her teeth.

"Well, it looks like we're partners then."

"Really?" Monica asked, sounding enthusiastic.

"Yeah." Elsa confirmed, a bit cold.

"Work together. You and me?" Monica asked, her enthusiasm replaced with suspiciousness.

"Yeah." Elsa confirmed again, though she sounded reluctant. Like Monica, Elsa rarely worked with other people, feeling she would get the work done faster if she did it by herself.

"You're serious?" Monica asked, her suspicion not calming down.

"Have you never partnered with anyone before?" Elsa asked sarcastically.

"Sure. I mean no. Wait. Hold on." Monica paused for a moment before confirming, "No. I haven't."

"Great." Elsa said sarcastically.

"You wanna start now? I was gonna head to the library." Monica asked, her enthusiasm returned. Elsa had to think about it for a second.

"Sure, I haven't seen the rest of this town. Lead the way."

"Great. Oh, and lucky for you, both the post office and the library have maps." Monica chuckled.

"Fantastic." Elsa sarcastically said before walking after Monica. Monica led Elsa past Bram's Costume shop on Burton Post Road, Elsa stopped for a second seeing the costumes hanging in the window. There was a cheerleader outfit that looked to be out of the Archie comics, colors matching and all. Though the top had some fake blood splashed on it, at least it looked like fake blood. A classic Frankenstein costume hung next to it, then a Werewolf costume, with some fake blood on the mouth of the mask, but the costume on the far end caught Elsa's eye. It wasn't that of a monster or any icon of Halloween, it was the most normal looking costume. Nothing more than a pair of white sneakers, blue jeans, and a gray hoodie. A hoodie with its front pocket nearly ripped from the seam, looking rather dirty on the shoulders.

"Hey!" Monica called. "You coming?" She asked. Elsa turned to her, "Yeah I was," Elsa looked back, but noticed something odd. The costume at the very end was gone. Elsa didn't know what to make of it. Her eyebrow raised like a goose bump.

"Admiring the costumes?" Monica asked. "Yeah. Yeah. They just caught my eye."

"I hear you; Mr. Bram makes all the best costumes." Monica stated.

"Makes?" Elsa asked.

"Oh yeah, Mr. Bram makes all the Halloween costumes by hand every year. You name it, he'll make it. Though he always has trouble making a Dracula mask. Something about never getting the teeth just right." Monica explained.

"Interesting." Elsa said, still looking at the empty spot in the window.

"Come on, the library's this way." Elsa just shook her head and walked after Monica.

✳✳✳

The library was two blocks down from Bram's Costume Shop, on Edgar Lane. Elsa looked at the building. It was a tall and wide brick building with seven stone steps out front. It looked somewhat small despite its length and width. A stone carving above the door looked to be depicting people standing around a stone book, that lay in the middle with EST. 1813 in the middle of the book's pages. It reminded

Elsa of Town Hall when she moved to town. Monica noticed Elsa's staring at the carving.

"If you're trying to figure out who the stone people are, don't worry they're Greek Gods." Monica chuckled.
"Which ones?" Elsa asked.

"I believe Zeus, Hera, Poseidon, Hercules, Narcissus, I think, and Apollo." Monica said. Elsa looked up at the stone god carvings. "Come on." Monica led Elsa inside.

The library door creaked like a haunted house as Monica opened it. Both doors did that, they weren't old or rusty, just in desperate need of some WD-40. The lights inside the library were dim, never being fully lit during the day. A cold draft wafted through the air. Elsa stepped further inside, seeing that the interior of the library was like the interior of her current home, larger on the inside than on the outside. There was no one in the library, at least no one either girl could see, so Elsa didn't feel so bad about uttering,
"Wow!" in a non-library appropriate tone.

"Shhh! Keep it down!" Monica whispered. Elsa looked at Monica with a confusing look, even with her glasses on. Monica couldn't contain her laughter as it snorted out of her nose. Elsa nodded her head, while playfully hitting Monica's shoulder.
"This place is huge." Elsa said, now maintaining a library appropriate tone.

"Bit different from looking at it outside huh." Monica stated.
"Yup." Elsa confirmed.

"You get used to it. Here in Steeple Hills, not everything is what it seems." Monica stated. Elsa shot Monica a look, but she didn't notice. Elsa began to wonder if there was more to this quiet little town.

The main desk of the library resided in the center of the room. A wide circular shape with an attached stand on the outside. Hundreds of books occupied the counter space, covering the desk's chipping black paint. Hundreds of newspapers crowded the inside of the desk area. One small golden bell lied on top of a thick book with a blood red spine. Monica looked around the counter before calling out,

"Mrs. Prenderghast!"

There was no answer.

"Weird. She's usually here." Monica said.

"Out for lunch maybe?" Elsa asked.

"She eats here." Monica said.

"Does she live here too?" Elsa sarcastically asked.

"Actually yes. She has an office apartment on the third floor." Monica confirmed. Elsa wasn't sure if Monica was joking or not. Monica placed her bag next to the bell's book and leaned over the counter, seeing more of the newspaper mess.

"Do you really think she's hiding under there?" Elsa asked. "Then again I haven't met the woman, so ignore what I said." She added, though Monica was already ignoring what Elsa asked.

In the midst of Monica's "search" for Mrs. Prenderghast, a bat flew down from the balcony of the second floor, quietly landing on Monica's bag. Elsa quickly noticed; her eyes widen in shock, though hidden behind her sunglasses.

"Uh Monica." She whispered so as to not to alert the bat.

"What's up?" Monica said, not moving from her leaning over.

"Um. Your bag."

"Why are you whispering?"

"On your bag." Monica stood up,

"What about my…. WHOA!" "AHHH!" The Bat spread its wings, let out a cry, and flew upward. It knocked the gold bell over in the process, it rang when it hit the floor. Monica's scream, and the ringing of the bell, seemed to be enough to attract Mrs. Prenderghast as she emerged from behind the stacks at the back of the library.
"I'm coming!" As Mrs. Prenderghast got closer, Elsa got a good look at what she looked like.

Mrs. Prenderghast was of a thin frame that could match Morticia Addams. She wore a checkered black and white dress with black boots that looked to be of a military style. Her face was semi-wrinkly with the hint of a chin whisker. She had thick framed glasses attached to a small chain that ran from ear to ear. Her hair was a bright silver, which seemed to go well with her light blue eyes.

"Oh Monica. It's you dear. Why did you scream? Rather loudly I should add." Mrs. Prenderghast asked, expressing some kind of accent that Elsa couldn't make out. Monica was near out of breath from her scream, holding her hand to her heart. She looked up towards the second floor's balcony. The balcony was long in length, there was a post top every twelve inches of the railing. Monica ran her eyes along the railing, passing one part of the railing with posts that had an inch between them. That's when she stopped and did a double take, "Him." Monica said, a bit angrily. Mrs. Prenderghast turned and looked at the balcony. She had this half-shocked look on her face while placing her hands on her hips, along with tapping her foot. "Bad boy Frankie." She said sternly.
"Frankie?" Elsa asked.

"Now you come down here this instant." Mrs. Prenderghast ordered. Frankie the Bat flew downward, landing on top of a thin stack of newspapers. "No, No Frankie." Mrs. Prenderghast yanked a medium-sized bronze cage out of the pile of newspapers near her right leg. She placed it on top of another pile of newspaper, which may or may not have looked like it was ready to tip over. She opened the little door, "In." She demanded. Frankie folded his wings like he was crossing his arms. "Don't you argue with me! I told you you're only allowed to fly around if you're not seen. Now please get in your cage." Mrs. Prenderghast politely demanded of her pet bat. Frankie shook his head. Mrs. Prenderghast began to get angry, arching her eyebrows downward so much that they almost vanished behind her glasses. Elsa took a step towards the desk.

"Does this usually happen?" She whispered to Monica.

"Honestly, no." Monica confirmed in a whisper. "Frankie's usually never out of his cage." Monica added. Elsa slowly looked at her with a confused look on her face, though Monica wasn't looking. Mrs. Prenderghast began tapping her long nails against the desk. The sound of her nails hitting the wood was rather loud and as Mrs. Prenderghast's boney fingers lifted then crashed into the wood, Frankie flinched every time. It wasn't so much the sound of the nails tapping on the wood that drove him crazy, for it pierced his ears harshly like a high-pitched whistle to the ears of a dog.

"Very well then. You win." Mrs. Prenderghast sighed in defeat. "For your victory, you will get a treat." Mrs. Prenderghast retrieved a small lunchbox from one of the desk's cubbies. She opened it, taking out a small container of mashed bananas. Frankie's eyes lit up as he saw the bananas. He practically drooled at the sight. Mrs. Prenderghast placed the container down, taking off the lid. The smell found itself in Frankie's nose and he basically dove for the bananas. He stuck his head into the container and began to devour the bananas. A sudden clang caught his attention.

It was at that moment that Frankie realized the clang, it was the closing and locking of his cage door. He looked up from his "victory treat", seeing Mrs. Prenderghast shaking her head with a sly smile on her wrinkly face. She had outsmarted him. "I can't believe you fell for that again Frankie." She said.

"Again?" Elsa asked.

"Oh yes dear, this is," Mrs. Prenderghast paused to think. "About the third time he's fallen for this." She confirmed. "And who might you be dear?" Mrs. Prenderghast asked, realizing the new face that is Elsa.

"Elsa Carlyle." Elsa said.

"She's new to town." Monica added.

"Well very nice to meet you dear, I'm the main librarian here in Steeple Hills. Carrigan Prenderghast." Mrs. Prenderghast held out her hand, which Elsa reluctantly shook. "Wait. Carlyle? Why have I heard that name before?"

"You may remember my grandparents more. Robert and Kathleen Walker?" Elsa said. The mention of Robert and Kathleen's names caused the bright silvery eyes of Mrs. Prenderghast to light up with shock.

"You're Robert and Kathleen's granddaughter?" She asked. Elsa nodded. "My word. That's WONDERFUL!" Mrs. Prenderghast screamed with excitement. "SSSSHHH!" Frankie alerted. "Oh, hush you!" Mrs. Prenderghast argued.

"You know dear. Your grandparents and I were friends for decades. I'm terribly sorry for their passing. They always came in here before closing and we have these talks reminiscing. Oh, how I miss those days." Mrs. Prenderghast spoke with a variety of emotions. "Yeah. I miss,"

"Wait then that means your mother is Wendy Walker?" Elsa again nodded. "Oh, that's lovely. I always had a feeling Wendy would move back home. Now you must have her come by; I'd love to speak with her again." Mrs. Prenderghast suggested.

"Sure. I'll get on that." Elsa said, though Mrs. Prenderghast missed the sarcasm that was attached.

"Now. What can I help you two with?"

"Well. Elsa and I are working together on a school project due on Halloween." Monica explained, breaking her silence. "Sounds splendid." "Now you wouldn't happen to have any books on the old grounds by the cemetery. Would you?" Frankie screeched wildly in his cage. Clearly mentioning the church angered him.

"Hush Frankie." Mrs. Prenderghast did her best to calm Frankie down. The girls didn't know what to make of Frankie's reaction, Elsa more than Monica. "Sorry about that. He gets a little jittery sometimes." "I guess mentioning the," Monica paused. "That place angers him?" She asked. Frankie's behavior was new to Monica. He had been Mrs. Prenderghast's pet for as long as Monica could remember and Frankie always seemed calm, aside from scaring people on occasion. "I guess so. He did used to live in there until," Mrs. Prenderghast hesitated to finish her sentence. Monica knew why.

"That's. Interesting." Elsa interjected, breaking the tension.

"Right, you are Elsa. It is quite interesting." Mrs. Prenderghast said, sounding eager to change the subject. "Now if you two are really interested in that subject, let me show you where those kinds of books reside." Mrs. Prenderghast walked out from the newspaper mess. Elsa now saw that the dress barely covered Mrs. Prenderghast's thick black boots, definitely looking to be of a military grade. Frankie watched, crossing his wings as the three women approached the spiral staircase.

Ascending the spiral staircase, Mrs. Prenderghast stopped on the seventh step and slammed her boot on it. "I really need to fix this step. Watch your footing." Despite the warning, Elsa still tripped going up. Frankie snickered in his cage.

"Shut up Frankie." Elsa whispered to herself, also wondering why she was semi-talking to a bat. Mrs. Prenderghast led the two girls towards the center of the second floor. The second floor continued the theme of deceiving looks of Steeple Hills. Elsa looked over the banister, seeing how the center desk looked like a giant pumpkin from above.

The second floor of the library looked larger than it would appear from below, allowing for ten full shelf stacks, with seven shelves on each stack. Ten tables occupied the center of the second floor, six of the tables has lamps in the center. Four chairs attached to each table.

Mrs. Prenderghast stopped, gazing at the second floor's ninth shelf unit. W/X was engraved in a silver plaque. "Ah. This is where you'll find it. Everything is in alphabetical order, oh what am I saying. Monica dear, you know how everything goes in here." Mrs. Prenderghast explained with a smile. "Indeed, I do." Monica replied with a smile of her own. "Well then, good luck. If you need anything, don't hesitate to ask." "Will do Mrs. Prenderghast. Thank you." Monica said. "Anytime dear." Mrs. Prenderghast said before walking away.

Monica dropped her bag onto the nearest table, at least the nearest one with a lamp. Elsa copied. "Ok so this is W/X, like Mrs.

Prenderghast said everything is in alphabetical order." Monica started.

"Great. Where's the ladder?" Elsa asked.

"Don't need one." Elsa followed Monica into the walkway between the stacks. "There aren't many books here that start with X."
"But apparently a lot that start with W." Elsa added with a tone of sarcasm.

"The title should have Whipstaff in it." Monica said, though she laughed a little at Elsa's sarcasm.
"Got it." The search for any book with Whipstaff in the title didn't last long, as no more than five minutes later Monica let out an "AH HA!" Monica's voice bounced off the stacks and the walls of the library, and she regretted it. A brief moment of silence fell upon the library. Frankie's snickering in his cage broke it.
"I'm gonna guess that means you found it?" Elsa asked sarcastically.

"Yeah!" Monica confirmed with some glee in her voice. Monica walked over to the table, placing the book down gently. It wasn't a thick-ish book but wasn't seen as thin either. Its cover the color of navy blue, the letting as white as bed sheets. Big white letters at the top read…

WHIPSTAFF
CEMETERY

Upon opening, a foul smell rose from the pages, reeking of old garbage and decay.
"Damn." Elsa waved her hand around, trying to swat away the smell.
"Old book."

"Clearly." Elsa cracked. Monica flipped through the pages, colored by age. Monica pushed the book closer to the lamp, seeing markings time had left on the pages of the book.

"Are we looking for anything specific?" Elsa asked.

"Ha." Monica said, keeping her discovery voice low.

"You're just gonna keep going with that aren't you?"

"Right here." Monica basically stabbed the page with her finger. Elsa looked at the page, the image of the cemetery was almost the same as it was when Elsa walked with Jack. "Old photo." Monica said.

"What gave it away? The smell of the page or the picture's white frame?" Elsa asked, which got a soft laugh out of Monica.

"Right here," Monica circled an area of the picture. "There's two crypts there now. This photo must've been taken before the tragedy." Monica explained.

"Tragedy?" Elsa asked, confused.

"Oh right. Forgot. You're still new here." Monica flipped to the next page; a picture of an old church filled the page. "The forest behind the cemetery, it wasn't always a forest. Then again, those grounds weren't always a cemetery." Monica started. "When Steeple Hills was started, it was a church ground. A large ground for a small church. It, Town Hall, and one other building are the last of the original buildings. As time went on, the yard was sectioned off to make room for the cemetery. Graves and bodies were moved from the forest, not a pretty sight I imagine. Eventually, the church was abandoned as the town progressed and more buildings were added. Everyone started going to the church over on Lee Drive. There were hundreds of plans to demolish it, but none ever went through." Monica explained.

"Why?" Elsa asked.

"Some say the place is haunted. Some say they can hear noises coming from inside the place. The main reason for demolishing it was because of its roof, but every mayor didn't have the heart to tear down a piece of the town's history. The debates went on for decades, and more or less are still going on." Monica explained.

"I'm guessing the church is still standing?" Elsa asked with unintentional sarcasm.

"Oh, it still stands, but twenty-five years ago, the church itself made the decision for them when part of the roof caved in…. with three high school students in there." Elsa looked at Monica.

"You're serious?" She asked. Monica nodded.

"It was horrible. Two seniors and one junior." She added.

"Whoa." Elsa said as Monica flipped the page, a newspaper clipping of the tragedy stapled to it. The headline read,

Three GHS students killed in Church roof cave in accident on Halloween!

Below the headline were black and white pictures of the church and two of the victims. "These are the two seniors." Monica pointed out. It was one male and one female. "Keith Maitland and Allie Crane." She added. "These two are the ones who have crypts in that space." Monica flipped back to the other picture. Elsa flipped back to the newspaper.

"Any id of the third victim?" She asked.

"No picture, but there is a name somewhere." Monica's eyes scanned the paper.

"Interesting. Wonder why he didn't mention that." She whispered, but Monica heard it.

"What is?" She asked.

"I walked by the cemetery yesterday. This guy Jack. I met him when I moved here. He showed me around and,"

"Showed you around. Do tell me more." Monica said jokingly.

"That was it. But he never mentioned this." Elsa finished, ignoring Monica's joke.

"Maybe he was related to one of those students."

"He did say he had close people in the cemetery."

"There you go. What was his name again?" Monica asked.

"Jack Harvey." Elsa said.

"Jack Harvey?" Mrs. Prenderghast emerged from the shadows of the staircase. "I haven't heard that name in a long time." She added.

"Yeah, Jack showed me around town yesterday." Elsa explained. Mrs. Prenderghast suddenly looked confused.

"Elsa dear, that's. Impossible." She said.

"Why?"

"On that night when that church caved in, Jack Harvey was the third student inside."

7
I see Dead People

Jack walked around Main Street. He slyly kicked some leaf piles as wind blew through, putting a small smile on his face. He played with some of the hanging pumpkins, lightly tapping to have them swing like pendulums. He jumped from the street to the curb and kept repeating it until he got to the bus stop, stopping in his tracks as the bus approached. He sat down next to an old lady with stringy red hair. "Afternoon Ms. Crenshaw." But Ms. Crenshaw didn't answer him. Jack dropped his smile. "Ok, looks like it's just one." Four other people walked up to the bus stop and boarded after Ms. Crenshaw. The bus driver closed the door and drove away. Jack looked at the clock above the post office across the street when he suddenly felt a slight pinch in his chest, he ran his hand over his heart, but the pinching didn't last. It wasn't the first time he had felt it, but he knew it never lasted long. He shrugged his shoulders and began to tap on his knees, tapping the melody of *The Addams Family*, snapping his fingers as well, then switching to *The Munsters*.

Elsa nearly fell over in shock, the feeling hitting her deep to her core. Monica helped her sit down. Mrs. Prenderghast had left to retrieve an old book from her desk area. She quickly returned with the book and a cup of water. "Here you go dear." Mrs. Prenderghast handed Elsa the water. Mrs. Prenderghast set the book down on the table. It was a thick-ish black book with blood red writing.

Gillman High School

The year was faded.

No smell escaped the book when it was opened. Mrs. Prenderghast flipped past the pictures of the faculty and administrators. "Here we are." She stopped on the pages that read...

IN MEMORY

Each picture was done in color. Keith and Allie's pictures were on top, next to each other. Keith's showing him in his basketball jersey, Allie in her cheerleading uniform. Jacks was on the bottom. It was a simple school photo, though Jack appeared to have a fat lip in it. It was the first time Elsa saw Jack without his hood on.

 "There's Jack Harvey." She said. Elsa took off her sunglasses, looking at Jack's picture for so long it would be considered studying. Jack's face was no different than when Elsa saw him.

"That's definitely him." She confirmed, her voice shaking a little.

    "Are you sure?" Monica asked.

"Monica, I am positive. That's the same guy I've been seeing since I moved here." Elsa said, she was beginning to get scared, and she didn't get scared easily.

    "This is very interesting." Mrs. Prenderghast observed, with a slight excitement in her voice. "No interesting doesn't sound right. This is astonishing." She added with further excitement.

"Yeah, I've been seeing a ghost." Elsa said, quite panicky.

    "Not just that. This means there is more to the story." Mrs. Prenderghast said. "What do you mean more?" Monica asked. "You see, no one ever knew why those three were in there that night. There were theories, hundreds of them actually. But nothing could ever be confirmed." Elsa suddenly felt overwhelmed, she chugged the glass of water, but it didn't seem to calm her down. Various thoughts ran through her mind, stabbing at her brain like knives into a piece of meat. "I knew something wasn't right." Mrs. Prenderghast wondered aloud. "Elsa. What else went on with Jack?" She asked as she propped herself onto the table. Despite this overwhelming, Elsa forced herself to speak. "He said all he does is walk around town. I saw him my first night, he was just kicking the leaf piles around."

"Leaf piles?" Mrs. Prenderghast asked.
"Yeah." Elsa said, despite sounding like she was babbling.

"That's interesting. Almost extraordinary." Mrs. Prenderghast stated. "How so?" Monica asked. "The leaf piles. Every year, just as they are cleaned up. They're kicked around moments later. During the day and the night. You say Jack walks around town all day and night. No one but you can see him. Then this means one thing." Mrs. Prenderghast explained.
"I've completely lost my mind?" Elsa asked, unable to contain her sarcasm.

"No. It means, we're looking at this wrong. We're looking at this as if Jack had suddenly returned from the great beyond. But judging from what you've said dear this means something else." Mrs. Prenderghast explained. "Like what?" Monica asked, slightly shaking with excitement.

"That Jack Harvey couldn't have returned, if he never truly left."

8
Make Yourself at Home

Jack remained at the bus stop. People came and went, but he never left. "Hey guys." He said as more people came for the approaching bus. But no one said a word back to him. He continued to tap on his knees, changing from *The Munsters* to the theme of *Scooby Doo, Where are you*. The bus arrived and more people got on and off. Jack stood up and stretched his legs and back. He sat down again and looked around, seeing no other bus in sight nor anyone else coming to the bus stop. He pulled his hood forward an inch, like he was trying to hide his face even more. He shifted his body until he was lying on his side, his legs hung over the edge. He pulled the strings on his hood, closing it until only his nose was "visible". He stuck his hand under right side of his hood covered face. This hand and hood combo became his pillow as Jack lied there, his eyes remaining open.

Elsa and Monica walked out of the library. Elsa didn't say a word as she walked ahead. Monica, however, had an excited smile on her face. She looked like a child opening a new toy on Christmas morning.

"This is awesome! I mean, I've had some weird experiences before, but nothing like this! This is amazing!" Monica said.
"Awesome? Amazing? Monica did you not hear Ms. Prenderghast?" Elsa asked, concerned about the situation.

"Ok first, it's Mrs. Prenderghast."
"Oh, excuse me." Elsa said.

"Second, I did hear her."
"Good, then you know that I'm,"

"You're communicating with a ghost. You're a medium!"

"A what?"

"A medium. A person who can communicate with the dead." Monica explained. "How are you not excited?" Elsa glared at her, unable to find the right words.

Elsa started to rub her forehead with the tip of her fingers.

"Let me guess, headache?" Monica said, unintentionally sounding sarcastic.

"What was your first clue?" Elsa asked angrily.

"You know, this is the second day I've known you and I'm just now realizing you have brown eyes." Monica quipped. Elsa quickly put her sunglasses back on, but her anger didn't fade, her sunglasses made her look even angrier.

"Look, maybe Jack had some relative that looks like him. It's not uncommon." Monica said, though she doubted it with every fiber of her being. Elsa rubbed her forehead again.

"Mrs. Prenderghast said Jack was the only child of an only child married to an only child," Elsa started, getting a bit frustrated with Monica.

"While that may be true, she also said Jack's parents lived by Whipstaff Cemetery." Monica explained. Elsa's anger turned into confusion.

"What's your point?" She asked.

"If you want answers about Jack Harvey. It wouldn't hurt to look at his house." Monica suggested, raising her eyebrow and smirking.

"Come on." Monica walked ahead.

"Or I could just find him and twist his neck until he speaks." Elsa said. She saw Monica run across the street, Elsa rolled her eyes and ran after her. Their backs turned to the library; a creature lurked behind the trees close to the library. Letting out a grunt like moan, the creature growled as it left deep claw marks in the nearest tree,

"New plan."

***

Elsa followed Monica all the way to Whipstaff Cemetery.

"This way." Monica walked around the cemetery. Elsa wanted to turn away and look for Jack, while also wanting to wring his neck, but Monica's insistence was too much to ignore. The situation of Jack being a ghost buzzed inside Elsa's mind like a bumblebee. She slowed down and looked at the cemetery, feeling drawn to it as if it were calling to her. She continued to walk forward until bumping into Monica, nearly knocking her over. "Hey." Monica said.

"Sorry." Monica could see the blank stare in Elsa's eyes.

"This ghost thing is really getting to you huh?" Monica asked, noticing Elsa's face, and continued staring at the cemetery. Elsa didn't answer. "Elsa!" That jerked Elsa back to reality.

"What?"

"I asked if this ghost thing was getting to you." Monica repeated.

"I never believed in ghosts."

"Guess you do now." Monica quipped.

"Why is this happening to me?" Elsa rhetorically complained, ignoring Monica.

"Genetics maybe?" Monica suggested.

"Oh yeah, like my mom can speak to ghosts and it just slipped her mind to tell me." Elsa retorted.

"Well not all genetic anomalies come from the mother." Monica retorted. Hearing that made any sarcastic remark in Elsa's head retreat. "Come on, the house is this way." Monica led on.
"How do you know that?" Elsa asked.

"When you and Mrs. Prenderghast were looking through the yearbook, I took a look at the newspaper clipping about the old church. Turns out it had all of Jack's information, but not his picture."
"Wait so it had his name and info, but not his picture?" Elsa asked.

"Actually, it didn't even have that at first. The article with the headline said third unidentified student. The second page identified him as Jack Harvey." Monica explained.
"Sounds like some reporter jumped the gun." Elsa noted.

"Sounds like it." Monica agreed. But then another thought join the thousands already running around in Elsa's mind.
"But that also means Jack's parents had to be called to the morgue to identify him." She said.

"Which sounds more like a bigger nightmare than anything on Elm Street." Monica quipped. "But anyway, it said that Jack lived with his parents at ninety-five Silberling place." Monica stopped at the top of Silberling place. It was a small and narrow street, with only four trees. Two with leaves, two without. "And it's right there." Monica pointed towards an old wooden house with a large front porch. It was one of seven houses on the street, the second house on the left side. It didn't match any of the other houses as it was devoid of any color. The other houses looked like they had been painted to match the colorful houses of *Edward Scissorhands*. Each house had a bright green lawn that looked freshly cut, but not a single car in any of the driveways. At least three of the houses showed crystal clear signs of being vacant, the other houses were unknown. A large yellow diamond shaped sign stood on Monica's right, which Elsa nudged her to look at.

It read simply.... **DEAD END**

"Well, that's," Monica started.
"Interestingly Ironic." Elsa finished, unintentionally sarcastic. Monica nodded in agreement. The two approached the house, though Elsa contemplated running into the cemetery to see if she could give Jack a second death.

A large brick chimney to the left. The roof looked to be missing one-third of itself due to a large hole. The sill below one window was crooked, looking like an upside-down evil eye. Most of the porch was plagued with cobwebs and rotting wood.
"Wow." Elsa said.

"Yeah. Bet when Jack lived here, it looked more alive." Monica quickly realized her poor choice of words. "That was bad. What do you think?" Monica asked.
"I think we're looking at the inspiration for the house from *Monster House*." Elsa cracked.

"You ready to go inside?" Monica asked.
"Is that rhetorical?" Elsa sarcastically asked, taking a step onto the porch.

Jack remained lying down on the bench. He sat up and pulled the hoodie hole open, exposing his face to the brisk air. As more people approached the bench, Jack started to lightly swing his head a little and tap his knees, deciding to tap the theme of *Casper the Friendly Ghost*. He didn't hum but kept replaying the lyrics in his head to keep pace.

Jack kept looking from left to right, seeing people cross the street, ignoring the flashing don't walk sign, the cars driving by, and some store owners re-hanging the Halloween streamers. He also saw Sheriff Pullman walk down the street, a bulky man whose age was no more than fifty-six, maybe fifty-seven. He kept scratching his forehead. Jack was halfway through tapping the song when he felt this tingling feeling in his head. He felt this tingle once before, his eyebrow arched, he stood up from the bench, panic growing on his face, and marched towards the cemetery.

Monica barely touched the rickety old door as it fell with a loud thud once it hit the floor, the hinges rusted to the point of breaking in half as the door fell. "Huh." She said. "Thought that be a little tougher." She added. Monica walked in first, Elsa slowly followed. The floorboards creaked under their feet. The interior was mainly dark except for a ray of light from the second floor. Monica turned on her cellphone's flashlight. She moved the light around like it was a scanner, looking over the room in front of her. Multiple pieces of furniture resided in the room, covered in white sheets. It appeared as a living room, the stairs running parallel to it. The situation of being inside Jack's house gave Elsa an eerie feeling, like a pit in her stomach. She copied Monica with her own cell phone flashlight.
"Why is the furniture still here?" Elsa asked.
"Don't know. It doesn't make sense why it would be just left behind after all these years." Monica observed.
"Unless they just left in the middle of the night and had no intention of remembering this town." Elsa cracked.

"Probably." Monica ignored part of the crack and lifted up one of the sheets. "AHHHH!" She backed away, screaming.

"What?" Elsa asked, nearly colliding into Monica.

Monica didn't scare easily, but whatever was under that sheet had her hand shaking. Elsa pulled off the sheet, revealing a wooden head on a wooden pole underneath. Perfectly shaped with dark brown hair, the red eyebrows were a big contrast. The left eye was green, the right was blue. Its nose was small, and its mouth hung open, almost as if it were broken.

"That is freaky." Elsa observed. She knelt down, moving closer to the head. She reached for it.

"What are you doing?" Monica asked. Elsa could hear the fear in her voice.

"What? Are you scared?" Elsa asked, a hint of sarcasm in her voice.

"No." Monica lied.

"Could've fooled me." Elsa sarcastically mumbled.

"Ok fine. I'll admit. I'm a little scared of puppets. Some dolls too." Monica admitted, though it sounded sarcastic. Elsa flashed Monica a look.

"Seriously?" She asked.

"Seriously." Monica confirmed.

It took Elsa a minute before she guessed "Slappy?"

"Chucky actually." Monica said. "But Slappy didn't help." She added.

"Ah." Elsa slowly picked up the head, rolling her eyes. "HHMPH." She said.

"What?" Monica asked.

"It's broken." Elsa said.

"How can you tell?"

"Simple. Have a look." She held the head in front of Monica's face. Elsa moved her thumb on the pole, nothing happened.

"Ok, It's definitely,"

"HELLO MONICA!"

The puppet head screamed.

"AAAAHHHHH!!!!!" Monica screamed.

"HAHAHAHAHAHAHA!" Elsa couldn't help but laugh. Monica caught on, real quick.

"That is NOT FUNNY!"

"Oh, come on. Let me have some fun in all this." Elsa said, cooling herself down from laughing.

"You know. You got a bit of an evil laugh. You know that?" Monica asked sarcastically.

"Yeah, I know." Elsa said with a smirk.

"Anyway, if you're done torturing me. Jack's room might be the best place to look for some answers." Monica suggested.

"Great." Elsa said, the urges to leave the house and to continue exploring fighting each other throughout her body, though she kept snickering before she tossed the puppet head back to the chair.

"Let's check upstairs." Monica said. She walked up the stairs first, each step creaking under her foot. The seventh step up let out a creek louder than the rest as Monica stepped on it. "Careful on that seventh step. I don't trust it." She said.

"I don't trust any of these," As Elsa stepped on the seventh step, it gave out. "AHHHHHH!"

"ELSA!" Monica reached out to grab her but missed as Elsa fell through the hole. She landed hard on her back. The broken step beside her. Elsa gazed up at the hole left of the step.

"Well. That sucked." Monica knelt down over the hole.

"ELSA!"

"I'm ok. For now, at least." Elsa pushed herself to stand up. She was lucky not to have broken her leg.

"Is that a closet?" Monica asked.

"I guess so." Elsa stepped on something hard. She leaned down, feeling the object. It was her phone. Picking it up, she sighed with relief the screen wasn't cracked, the flashlight was still lit. She looked around the room, seeing mounds of dust, extra white sheets, and the broken stick of a broom.

"Definitely a closet." She confirmed.

"Try and find a door. It doesn't look like that big of a room."

"You're not the one in it." Elsa angrily spoke through her teeth. The light caught the shine of a doorknob, right in front of Elsa.

She barely touched the knob as the door fell forward, crashing to the kitchen floor. "Not my fault." She mumbled. The kitchen was dark like the living room, only source of light was the light from the windows and with the heavy blinds still attached, it was extra thin light. Elsa returned to the steps,

"Ok this time, I'm definitely avoiding the seventh step." She angrily said, though it sounded like a joke.

"Wouldn't have it any other way." Monica quipped. "Is your leg, ok?" Monica asked.

"Yeah. Painful, gonna have to come up with something good for the bruise." Elsa stated.

"You bruise that easy?"

"No, just covering my bases." Despite the pain in her leg, Elsa climbed the stairs again. Elsa leaped over the seventh step. "Ok. Let's get moving." Elsa walked forward and Monica followed.

Jack appeared on Silberling Place. He shook his head at the sight of the dead-end sign. He saw his house; the open front door was hard to miss. Jack looked back at the cemetery, then back at his house. He shook his head again and went to the front door. His hands shook at the threshold. He shook his head again, "No. No." He walked to the broken bench on the porch and sat down, a mix of embarrassment and shame tingled in his body. "Ok. Let's see who was dumb enough to go in this time."

The upstairs hallway felt less eerie than the living room, despite the reflections of the flashlights. Three holes marked the ceiling, it appeared there were hanging lights there at one point. "I can hear the bugs in the walls." Monica said. Elsa looked back at her, "Never mind." Monica said. "Can you see anything with those sunglasses on?" Monica asked.

"I can see just fine." Elsa said, rather quick, like she was expecting Monica to ask. While the hallway was cold and, how Elsa didn't want to be in the house, she couldn't help but feel somewhat pulled towards the end of the hallway.

"Hey, over here." Elsa turned seeing Monica in front of a door. Monica looked inside. Elsa stood in the doorway while Monica entered the room. It was average size for a bedroom. Several floorboards were missing. Three pieces of furniture remained, much like the living room furniture, they were covered in sheets. Monica looked under the sheets, seeing two rocking chairs and a bedframe, albeit a broken one.

"This is Jack's room?" Elsa wondered. Monica looked around; Elsa found the closet. Inspecting the inside, she swatted away hundreds of cobwebs. At first glance, it looked small, but looking to the left of the closet it extended another five feet. The cell flashlight caught sight of a plastic covered suit. Elsa pulled it forward, Monica joined her.

"Find anything?" She asked.

"Yeah." Elsa pulled the suit out of the closet. Monica ran her fingers along the plastic, noticing the dust sticking to her fingers. She unzipped the plastic bag, feeling the suit inside. The threads came apart at the touch of her fingers.

"Ozzy and Sharon." Elsa cracked.

"Ok. This must be his parents' room." Monica observed. "Clearly." Elsa zipped up the bag and hung it back in the closet, quickly shutting the door to it. "Come on." "Seriously who leaves their wedding clothes behind?" Elsa asked, not caring that she wasn't gonna get that answer.

Monica and Elsa walked out of the room, slowly shutting the door behind them. Sudden whispering caught Elsa's ear. Elsa found herself drawn to the sound.

"Elsa?" Elsa didn't hear Monica, the whispering grew louder with almost every step Elsa took, but it was semi-inaudible. She rounded a corner at the end of the hallway, seeing a closed door at the end. The shiver in Elsa's spine grew as she crept towards the door. She felt a buzzing in the back of her head as she reached for the door, it was as if her conscience was saying "Don't open the door".

"What's the matter?" Monica asked.

"Do you hear that? The whispers?" Elsa asked, sounding like she was in a trance.

"What whispers?" Monica asked, concern growing within her body.

Elsa turned the knob, pushing the door open. The room was dark, windows appeared non-existent. Monica followed Elsa as she walked inside. The whispers grew as the girls entered, beginning to sound like multiple voices at once. Elsa couldn't make out a single word they were saying, but they were starting to test the patience of Elsa's eardrums. Unlike the other bedroom, this room was completely empty. No white sheet covered furniture, no hint that anyone ever occupied the room.

The heavy blinds shot up like rockets, revealing two large windows. Elsa and Monica nearly had simultaneous heart attacks. Monica clutched her chest just like before.

"You, ok?" Elsa asked, feeling her heart in her throat.

"Yeah. It's just." Monica paused. She took several deep breaths, still clutching her chest. "My heart just skipped a beat for a second." She explained.

"Really?" Elsa asked. "Cause you look like you got the ever-living sh-,"

"I appreciate the concern. But I'm ok." Monica bluntly said. Elsa sensed Monica was hiding something. Monica inspected the blinds,

"Elsa?"

"Yeah?"

"Are we the only ones in the room?" Monica asked. Elsa looked around, seeing only Monica.

"Yeah." She confirmed. "Why?"

"Because these blinds wouldn't just shoot up on their own. Wasn't sure if someone yanked them down to send them flying." Monica explained.

"Well doesn't look like there are any ghosts in here. Wait," Elsa suddenly noticed how quiet the room had gotten. "There isn't anything in here. I can't hear the whispers anymore."

"What did they say anyway?" Monica asked.

"There was multiple, all speaking at once, like they were arguing." Creaking of the floorboards alerted the two. "Ok, I know this was my idea. But as cool as this is, I think we need to get out of here." Monica noted.

"Yeah. After you."

"Oh, thank you." Monica said sarcastically. Monica ran out first, but a hanging picture on the back of the door caught Elsa's eye. It was in a wooden frame with a thin piece of glass protecting the picture. Elsa unhooked it, lifting up her glasses to read it,

From childhood's hour I have not been
As others were -- I have not seen
As others saw -- I could not bring
My passions from a common spring --
From the same source I have not taken
My sorrow -- I could not awaken
My heart to joy at the same tone --
And all I lov'd -- I lov'd alone --
Then -- in my childhood -- in the dawn
Of a most stormy life -- was drawn

That's where the poem stopped, it seemed familiar to Elsa, but she couldn't remember from where she had seen it. Elsa took off her glasses as she looked at the back of the frame, finding words written with what appeared to be, a black marker.

Your favorite poem Jack.
In case you find your way home
I'm Sorry Son. We love you.
Rest in Peace.

The word peace had some dripping under it, whoever had written it clearly had started crying while writing it. Elsa snapped a picture, then hung the picture back on the door. She wiped away the hint of a tear and covered her eyes with her sunglasses again.

"Elsa!" Monica called. She hadn't realized Elsa wasn't behind her. Elsa tucked away her phone and walked out of the room; the floor continued to creak under her feet. Elsa wondered if the floor was going to give out as the creaking got louder.

"Stay Away!"

Something whispered in Elsa's ear. She jerked her head around, seeing no one behind her. All she saw was the darkness of the hallway, illuminated by the bright light of her phone.

"Stay Away!"

The voice repeated.

"Stay Away!"

The sound of creaking ceased, the sound of footsteps replacing it. Elsa moved forward. Against her better judgement she uttered, "Who's there?"

"STAY AWAY!"

A strong force sent Elsa flying backwards, landing on her back. Elsa briefly looked up, seeing no one. She pushed herself to stand up, but the floor beneath her gave out, "AHH!" Her scream was muted by her hitting the floor, landing on her side.

"ELSA!" Monica ran over to her. "Oh my god, are you ok?" She asked. Elsa didn't respond, pain shooting through her body. "Ow." That was all escaped her mouth. "Note to self, never say who's there." She mumbled as Monica helped her stand up.

"I know this is a bad time but, I feel like this, and the stairs are karma for the puppet,"

"Monica. Do me a favor."

"What?"

"Bite me!"

"Come on."

They were nearly blinded when they got outside, from complete darkness to light wreaked havoc on their eyes, even through Elsa's sunglasses. The flashing lights on the police car didn't help either. Sherriff Pullman got out of the car. "Sheriff Pullman?" Monica asked, she couldn't see him clearly. "Hello Monica." Sheriff Pullman said, his deep voice sounding like he spoke through a megaphone. "You two are in a lot of trouble."

9

Nevermore

It was around five o'clock when Sheriff Pullman pulled up to Elsa's house. Wendy stood on the front porch with Lieutenants Esteves and Addams. Sheriff Pullman opened the backdoor, allowing Elsa out first. She wasn't handcuffed, but the feeling of sitting in the back of a police car felt the same, handcuffed or not. Elsa knew she was in a lot of trouble as she limped to the door.

"Oh, thank god." Wendy came rushing down the lawn, hugging Elsa tightly, the pain in Elsa's body became excruciating. When she let go, she noticed the pain in her daughter's face. "Are you alright?"

"A little banged up and maybe bruised." Elsa said, wincing in pain.

"I take it my lieutenants have kept you company?" Sheriff Pullman joked. "Yes, they have. Thank you." Wendy confirmed. "What happened exactly?" She asked. "Elsa, is it?" Sheriff Pullman asked.

"Yes sir." Elsa confirmed, for she was more focused on the pain than being sarcastic at the moment.

"Well Elsa here was with Monica King," Sheriff Pullman pointed to the back of his car, showing Monica sitting with her head down. "Now we had gotten a report of two young girls breaking into one of the old houses over on, huh."

"Silberling." Elsa interjected.

"Thank you. On Silberling place. Now the house has been vacant for quite a while," "Breaking in?" Wendy looked at Elsa, furious, but kept it calm in front of Sheriff Pullman.

"It wasn't like that. It was for our school project; we needed a closer look at the house. The front door just fell inward when we got on the porch. We never even touched the door." Elsa explained.
"Wait which house was it?" Wendy asked, an old memory coming to mind.

"Ninety-five," Elsa confirmed, Wendy's anger grew.
"That house?" Wendy asked. Sheriff Pullman was interested by both Elsa's explanation and Wendy's reaction. "Mrs. Carlyle, may I speak with you privately?" "Of course. Elsa inside." Wendy said sternly. Elsa didn't say anything as she sadly and painfully walked inside, knowing this wasn't going to get much better.

Wendy watched as she closed the door. She looked back at Sheriff Pullman. "Wendy, I take it you remember." Sheriff Pullman noted, his hands placing themselves on his hips, getting slight pain in his left hip. "Oh, I remember. I was seventeen and a senior when it happened." Wendy confirmed. "Look whatever the charges,"

"There are no charges. Not sure if you remember. But no one has heard from Johnny and Winona Harvey in over twenty years. The town owns the house now. Mayor Stein intends to donate the stuff inside by Christmas. He wants the whole street demolished by Valentine's Day." Sheriff Pullman explained. "The whole street?" Wendy asked.

"No one has lived on Silberling since that night. The Harvey's were the last couple to leave. Now if your daughter says the door fell inward, I believe her. I just don't want her, or anyone else for that matter, near that house. One day, that house is gonna collapse like the old church. I don't want anyone else getting killed." Sheriff Pullman explained. "Oh, believe me Sheriff. Elsa won't be stepping near, let alone inside, that house anytime soon." Wendy stated. In all the years he had known her, Sheriff Pullman never had a reason to doubt Wendy. "Good to know. Wendy, let me tell you something. Monica King, she's a good kid. She's just had it rough most of her life. Never had any real friends. I think your daughter might be her first." Sheriff Pullman explained, while Wendy eyed Monica in the backseat of the police car.

"Yeah, Elsa's no different in the friend's department." Wendy admitted. Though she was still furious, a small part of her was happy Elsa was hanging around with other people. "Anyway, you have yourself a good night, Wendy." "You too Sheriff." Wendy said as Sheriff Pullman tipped his hat, "Oh and Wendy." He called. "Welcome home. I'm sure your parents would be happy to see you back in this house." He added. Wendy smiled, "Thank you." Sheriff Pullman got back into his car and drove away. The Lieutenants left as well, waving goodbye to Wendy as they left Spellman Dr. Lieutenant Addams appeared to smile at her as they drove away.

Wendy walked inside, loudly closing the door behind her. Elsa sat at the kitchen table, her sunglasses on the table. She held an ice pack to her side and placed another one under her leg. Walking into the kitchen,

"Mom," Wendy stopped Elsa before she could explain. "Two ice packs?"

"Like I said I'm a little banged up." Elsa said, almost in complete pain.

"You got lucky that the Sheriff isn't pressing charges. Neither is the family,"

"Well, the family abandoned the house so," It took one angry look from Wendy to zip Elsa's lip.

"Doesn't matter. What were you really doing in there?" Wendy asked, now curious of her daughter's actions. She knew Elsa didn't want to move to Steeple Hills but breaking and entering was not something she ever thought her daughter would do, as far as she knew.

"Like I said, it was for our school project. Ms. Shelley partnered Monica and I and we wanted some authenticity for the project."
"Ok, then I take it this was that girl Monica's," Wendy started.

"Nope, All my idea." Elsa said. Wendy wanted to believe Elsa, but there was something deep down telling her Elsa was just covering, though she felt slightly proud, she was still furious.
"Noble. But you're still grounded." Elsa dropped her head. "So, you won't be going anywhere else but here and school. This project, work on it with Monica the best you can at school. No visitors. Understood?" Wendy said, sternly.

"Yeah." Elsa agreed, it was better for her to agree to that than make the situation worse. She knew Wendy wouldn't believe her about Jack.

"Now, straight upstairs!" Wendy ordered. Elsa stood up, leaving the ice pack for her leg on the chair. She walked upstairs, keeping an ice pack against her side. Wendy watched as Elsa went into the hall and vanished from sight. She gazed over at the fireplace, then walked into the living room. Several pictures lined the mantel. One to the far right was a picture of her mother, holding baby Elsa. Wendy took a close look at her mother in the picture. She was smiling and had it looked like she had a tear in her eye. "If only you were still here. I could really use your guidance right now mom." She took the picture, holding it tightly in her hands, she looked at the stairs then back at the picture.

A cold sensation hit Wendy's shoulder, she looked behind her, seeing one of the living room windows was still open. Wendy put the picture back on the mantel, then slammed the window shut. She left the living room, unaware of the pictures of her mother watching her every move and mouthing "Just Like Me!"

✳✳✳

In the middle of the night, Elsa lied in her bed, unable to sleep. The ice pack had melted, now residing on a towel on the floor. The day's events running around in her head like a zombie chasing a human. She turned, lying on her back, staring up at the ceiling. Lying there uncomfortably, she tossed the pillow beneath her head to the floor, dropping her head onto the sheet covered mattress. She closed her eyes, but sudden tapping forced them back open.

Elsa slowly got out of bed, checking on the stairs that lead to her room. The bedroom door was left open, a part of her grounding. She checked the smaller sized windows, which were slightly cracked open, but found nothing. She heard the tapping again, Elsa turned towards the larger window, Wendy had replaced the original orange curtains with dark red ones. Elsa cautiously walked over to the window, pushing the curtains aside, she saw nothing but the crescent moon in the sky. "What the,"

Jack leaped into view. "AH!" Elsa squeaked, and she mentally questioned herself for it. "Jack?" He waved. Elsa opened the latch on the window, pushing it open, allowing Jack to enter.

"Sorry about the scare." He said.

79

"Keep your voice down." Elsa warned, though she quickly remembered her current situation.

"Sorry." Jack whispered.

"What are you doing here?" Elsa asked. Jack looked at Elsa,

"Huh." He said, somewhat amazed.

"What?"

"I just realized. I, uh, never saw your eyes before. They're nice." He said.

"Jack." She said angrily.

"Right. Not the time."

"Why are you here?"

"Oh no. I'm asking you the questions first. Namely, what were you doing in my house?" Jack asked, sounding a bit angry. Elsa was shocked to hear that from him. In the brief time she had known him, he appeared as someone who could never be angry for anything.

"You knew?"

"I was there Elsa." Jack admitted. "I was sitting on the porch." He said.

"When? I didn't see you."

"When you and that other girl got arrested." Jack confirmed. "You never looked my way." He added.

"So, it wasn't you then." Elsa noted.

"What wasn't me?"

"The. The thing that sent me falling through the floorboards." Elsa explained.

"You fell through the floor! Are you ok?" Jack asked.

"Some bruising but I'll get over it." Elsa said, feeling the stinging of pain in her leg and side.

"Ok? But that wasn't me. I didn't go inside." Jack confirmed. "Wait, you didn't answer my question. Why were you in my house?" Jack asked. "Also, what happened to the seventh step?" He added. "It broke when I stepped on it." Elsa said.

"Geez, did you fall through that too?" Jack asked. "Yes, I fell!" Elsa snapped.

"Ok. Sorry I asked." Jack said, a hint of regret in his voice. "Wait you said you didn't go in." Elsa noted.

"Elsa, I don't need to go inside to see the staircase. Also why did you knock the door down?"

"It fell on its own. We barely touched it." Elsa argued. "Anyway, Monica and I were in the house because we," Elsa hesitated.

"We what?" Jack asked.

"We were looking for answers or clues. We didn't get any." Elsa confessed.

"Clues to what?" Jack asked.

"Your death."

Jack's face went pale, even for his current situation, and his eyes shot open. He placed his hand over his mouth and inhaled, courting a bit of a snort. He started taking slightly deep breaths.

"How do you know about that?" He asked, moving his hand to the top of his hood.

"Mrs. Prenderghast told me." Elsa explained.

"Ah she's always been a sweet woman." Jack said, his deep breathing charting the territory of hyperventilation. "So, she told you everything? Me, Keith, and Allie?" He added.

"We didn't have enough time for the whole story. We were busy looking into you being a ghost." Elsa angrily quipped. "Oh, by the way." Elsa punched Jack's shoulder; she was surprised her hand didn't faze through.

"OW!" He said. "What was that for?" He asked. Elsa looked at him angrily.

"You know damn well what that was for." She stated. Jack sighed.

"I take it I should fill in some blanks."

"Well, it would certainly help." Elsa said angrily.

"Alright. Ok. Here it goes. I grew up with Keith Maitland and Allie Crane. They made my life hell. I'll spare you elementary and middle school. Now in high school, Keith was on the Gillman basketball team. He was made captain our freshman year. He was horrible. An arrogant jerk with zero talent on the court. He thought he got away with a lot because he was the, watch my hands, 'star'." Jack used air quotes when saying star. "But his teammates said otherwise. They tried a few times to get him kicked off the team. But those pleas fell on deaf ears. Keith thought he was untouchable. Allie initially was just another bully, but she became Keith's girlfriend in seventh grade and in high school she was the head cheerleader, you know that old cliché."

Elsa nodded for she hated that cliché herself. "She was also the basketball coach's niece. The daughter he never had. An outright entitled princess. Just as arrogant and selfish as Keith, but a bit more delusional. I say, just maybe ten percent more delusional. I never knew why, but for long as I've known him, Keith always preferred to pick on me. No one ever helped me, they just laughed or kept walking and pretended nothing was going on. It came to a point where I just never really went anywhere after school or even wanted to go to school. I just went straight home and stayed there." Jack explained.

"Jack. What exactly happened that night?" Elsa asked, the pain in her body forcing her to sit on the edge of her bed.

"Like I said, I just stayed home. I didn't have," Jack paused. "Friends. Well not human friends. Just Boris." He admitted.

"Boris?" Elsa asked.

"My dog. You know, Man's best friend. He was given to me for my fifteenth birthday. He got out a lot because my dad had a habit of leaving the front door open. But Boris always came back. He loved playing hide and seek." Jack explained, a somber tone in his voice as his reflections flashed in front of him. "My dad saw him as a way to get me out of the house. He got annoyed that I was home every weekend in High School." Jack explained. "Always said, 'You're in high school now Jack, get out there and mingle, but stay out of trouble'." Jack saw his father's face flash before him, but he quickly pushed it away.

"Is that why you were at the church that night?" Elsa asked.

"Truth be told, my dad kinda forced me to go out. I tried my best not to be seen, but Keith and Allie managed to find me. Keith nearly made me pass out when he dragged me to the old church. Nearly gave me a concussion when he threw me to the ground. He was angrier than usual with me that day." Jack explained.

"Why?" Elsa asked. Jack sighed.

"I may or may not have punched him in the face earlier that day." Jack said sheepishly.

Elsa's eyebrow shot up, "Oh really?"

"It was an accident. He was messing with me, and I don't know what came over me. But next thing I know he's down on the ground with a bloody nose and his blood's on my fist." Jack explained.

"So, Keith wanted revenge." Elsa deduced.

"Like all bullies, Keith didn't like it when anyone stepped up to him. So, when I tried in the church, I got punched in the jaw, multiple times. Sometimes I still feel the stinging. Allie just stood there laughing and cheering him on. I tried to fight back, but Keith just kept wailing on me. Punch after punch, kick after kick. I remember the taste of blood in my mouth, the feeling of Keith's fist probably breaking my nose, and the buzzing feeling I got when he kicked me in the stomach." As Jack explained, the images of that night flashed in front of him. He heard Keith's grunting and Allie's cheering of "GET HIM KEITHY!" in his ears.

"But then Boris came running in, he scared the daylights out of Allie. Keith screamed, I'm not entirely sure, but I think Boris may have bit Keith in the leg. Then I remember Boris looking up and barking. I tried to warn them, but they didn't want to hear it. I reached for Keith, but then the place caved in. Everything went dark after that." The images flashed before him again, Boris' barking and Allie's screaming hot his eardrums hard like a hammer hitting a nail.

"When my vision came back, I found myself waking up in the cemetery like," Jack paused. "I guess the next day."
"When did you realize,"

"That I was dead? For a minute or two I thought I was dreaming or that I somehow miraculously survived untouched. I almost had myself fooled until I saw one of my sneakers left in the rubble. Believe me it wasn't easy coming to terms with being a ghost." Jack explained. "Got even worse when my parents left town. Just up and left. Just made me feel more alone in death than I did in life."
"That would explain why some furniture is still in there." Elsa said.

"Yeah. Something tells me they were gonna come back for it, but just never did." Jack explained, retaining the somberness to his voice. "But twenty-five years later I'm surprised that stuff is still in there." He added.

"Well. Your parents left something for you." Elsa opened her phone gallery, bringing up the poem.

"Huh?"

"Here. Two pictures." Elsa handed Jack the phone, he stared at the poem for a moment, then scrolled to the next. Seeing the message from his parents stirred a feeling in Jack, one he hadn't felt in a long time.

"Never knew they were paying that much attention." Jack handed the phone back to Elsa, constantly blinking his eyes, but failing to hide the mistiness in them.

"So are all four of you ghosts then, I guess the others don't feel like leaving the cemetery?" Elsa asked.

"Actually, just me." Jack confirmed.

"What about Keith and Allie?" Elsa asked.

"No idea. I've never seen their ghosts, but their bodies are in their crypts. I've seen them."

"And Boris?" The images flashed before him once more,

"Well, once I realized what happened, I checked around the church. Aside from the police tape, I saw a few paw prints in the dirt. Since no one in town ever took their pets for a walk there I initially thought they were Boris'. Made me think he got out somehow. But I found out the prints belonged to the police dogs, I guess they were used in searching the rubble. I would love to believe Boris got out. But whether he did or out, I never saw him again." Jack explained.

"So what? You've just been walking around town for the last twenty-five years because you wanted to?" Elsa asked.

"Well, I didn't want to spend every moment in the cemetery. It's a little grim. To be honest, Elsa. I'm not sure why I haven't crossed over. Hard to think if my parents are on the other side. As bad as it's going to sound, I'm pretty sure Boris is on the other side. I'm not sure why I'm not! But,"

"But what?" Elsa asked.

"Ok. I don't just kick the leaves on main street. I basically go around every street and last night I was on this street. No leaf piles by the way. But when I went to walk back," Jack stopped, trying to find the right words.

"What?" Elsa asked, growing a little impatient.

"Something called my name." He said, sounding like he had to force the words out.

"Called your name?" Elsa asked, clearly confused. "Is that how you ended up in the window of the costume store?" Jack suddenly felt embarrassed.

"No, that was an accident. I was just walking around, and I wanted to see what other costumes Mr. Bram was making. I only meant to poke my head in, but then I saw you coming, and I ducked inside. It wasn't my brightest move I'll admit." Jack explained, sounding more ashamed than embarrassed with himself. "But back to the thing calling my name. I think there's something out there. Something that,"

"Could've been what sent me through the floorboards." Elsa realized.

"After you what've mentioned, probably. But whatever it is. I don't know. I just want to crossover." Jack said.

"You really want to be out of here that bad?" Elsa asked, standing up.

"Coming from the woman who doesn't want to be in this town."

"Touché."

"Honestly Elsa, I got nothing left here." Jack expressed. "Don't get me wrong. I'm born and raised here. I love this town, but I just feel it's time to move on." He added. "But here I am, twenty-five years later. I still got nothing." He added. "Nothing in life, nothing in the afterlife." He stated. "Actually, I'm wrong. Only thing I got is this." Jack stepped into the beam of moonlight coming from the window. "Ever seen *Curse of the Black Pearl*?" Jack asked as Elsa saw his body became transparent and glowing blue.

Elsa stared at Jack's transparent form. He stepped back, his glow fading, and his body became full once more. Elsa stood up and stepped closer to Jack. She reached for his hood, "Hey."
"Oh please. Consider us even with this." She gently pulled his hood back, revealing his dark hair. Elsa could feel the chill between the two of them.

"Even for what?"
"You saw my eyes. Now I've seen your hair." Elsa argued.

"Oh." Jack said stepping back from Elsa's hands, leaving his hood down. "Anyway, for the last twenty-five years, I've basically been invisible."
"I can see that." Elsa quipped.

"You're clearly the only one that can. You know that whole, a ghost can appear and disappear whenever they want thing?"
"Yeah?"

"Yeah, I can't do that." Elsa arched her eyebrow. "Yeah so, I'll be seeing you and vice versa, tomorrow and probably every day until the trumpets sound or until you leave." Jack said as he climbed to the window, Elsa could hear the defeat in his voice. She understood it wasn't his fault he was stuck in limbo, forced to endure being in Steeple Hills instead of possibly being with his family on the other side.

"Hold up." Jack looked back from the window. "This goes against how angry I am at you; how angry I am living in this town. But I'm gonna help you."

"What?" Jack asked, looking at her with a surprised yet puzzled look on his face.

"You heard me." Elsa smirked.

"Elsa, you don't have to. Also, I'm not sure how you can, unless you have some Ghostbuster DNA in you." Jack said. Elsa shot Jack a look, he quickly realized she wasn't changing her mind. He sighed. "But you're going to anyway." Elsa nodded. "Fine. Meet me at the cemetery tomorrow. I guess after school for you."

"Done."

10

Scream Team

Elsa awoke the next morning, the images of Jack's death still fresh in her head. "Good morning." Wendy stood at the top of the stairs,

"Were you watching me sleep? Very creepy."

"Forgot to mention. I'll be driving you to school today." Wendy said, ignoring Elsa's question.

"You have to be kidding."

"Do I look like I'm kidding?" Wendy asked. Elsa mentally gave the round to Wendy.

"I'll be down in a minute." Wendy left the room; Elsa knew getting past her after school was going to be tough. But she was determined.

As she stood up and stretched, she noticed a picture of her grandmother holding baby Elsa on the floor, just under the note that read, Or Here!. It was propped up to face Elsa's bed as if it was watching her. She picked up the picture, knowing she didn't put it there. She stared at it in a groggy confusion, for a brief moment, she wondered if she had slept walked and brought the picture up. But she knew she had a much more important matter at hand. "Ellie! Get a move on!" Elsa rolled her eyes before she grabbed her jeans and jacket from her closet and slammed the door shut.

＊

Wendy watched Elsa walked to the front doors of Gillman, it was part of Elsa's grounding. Elsa's grogginess from last night had not faded, she kept her sunglasses on to keep the sun from stinging her now bloodshot eyes. Though she couldn't do much about the pounding in her head. Walking inside, Elsa noticed Monica waiting by the lockers.

"Hey. There you are." She said, seeing Elsa approach.

"Here I am." Elsa said, rather tiredly.

"You get in trouble?" Monica asked.

"Grounded until next week. You?" Elsa asked.

"Grounded until Thanksgiving."

"Ouch." Elsa said, now she felt like she was boasting of her short grounding.

"Yeah well. Like I said in the car, not the first time Sheriff Pullman has driven me home."

"Well, someone's more of a bad girl than she looks." Elsa quipped.

"I try." Monica joked.

"What are you doing after school?" Elsa asked.

"Home why?" Elsa pulled Monica aside.

"No, you're not. I need your help."

"With what? We still have the project,"

"Forget about the project. Jack Harvey showed up in my room last night."

"HE WHA,"

"SSSSHHHH!" Elsa covered Monica's mouth, which did garner a few looks from the other students. "He showed up in my room, a little ticked we went in his house. I told him I would help him. I'm meeting him after school at the cemetery. You in?" Elsa explained, removing her hand from Monica's mouth.

"Help him with what?" Monica asked.

"It's a long story. You in or out?" Elsa asked, rather harshly.

"It's cheesy, isn't it?" Monica asked.

"Does that matter?" Elsa asked.

"Nope. I'm in." Monica said, nearly brimming with excitement. "Good. Now, unfortunately," The bell rang loudly, echoing inside and out of Gillman.

"We have class."

"Yup."

Monica and Elsa walked towards the classroom. Several students looked at them, some murmuring, and some just uttering whisper like laughter. Elsa knew Hunter had something to do with it because she did hear the name Eerie Elsa get dropped.

When they turned toward Ms. Shelley's classroom, Elsa bumped into a student, nearly falling over.

"Sorry." The student turned around.

"Oh, hey Finn." Monica sounded glad to see him. "Hey Monica." Finn said. "How you doing?" "I'm good. How about you?" "I'm good. You look like you haven't slept." Monica quipped. "I haven't actually." Finn said, slightly grinning. He looked at Elsa. "Sorry about bumping you."

"Oh no, completely my fault. I wasn't looking." Finn said. "I'm Finn Deetz."

"Elsa Carlyle. I think we have English together." Elsa smiled. Finn had to think about it for a moment. Marcus came out of nowhere, slamming his arm around Finn in a friendly manner. "Sorry about that. My cousin tends to forget somethings." Finn looked at him, his eyes squinted.

"Marcus Deetz." Finn pushed Marcus' arm off.

"Elsa Carlyle."

"Nice to officially meet you, new girl, and yes Finn we do have English with her. Much like we have history with Monica." "You have history with Monica, I have gym with her." "Oh, that you remember." Finn just shook his head, feeling this was another one of Marcus' attempts to set him up with a date. Marcus always played Finn's wingman, even if Finn told him not to.

"How are you guys coming on your project?" Monica asked. "Oh, we're doing just fine." Marcus boasted. He didn't seem arrogant, just a bit overconfident. "And by we, he means me." Finn said. "Oh, come on cuz. You and I are a good team when it comes to projects." Marcus said. "Yeah. I do all the work and you just put your name on it." Finn quipped. Marcus looked at Finn, coping the eye squinting. Finn smiled in a sarcastic manner. Marcus looked at Elsa and Monica. "Heard Ms. Shelley paired you two up. How are you coming along?" He asked. "Good. I think we're on page," Monica paused. "Where did we stop yesterday?" She asked Elsa.

"Page twenty-six I think." Elsa lied.

"Already?" Marcus complained.

"What can we say?"

"We surprisingly work well together." Monica added, though Elsa found herself reluctant to agree with it. Marcus looked at Finn.

"You need to work faster." He said. "What?" Finn complained. "Sleepy head over here stopped at ten pages." "Oh, shut up." "How are we gonna pass with only ten pages?" Marcus complained. "I wasn't stopping at the ten,"

"This is where we take our leave. See you guys in class." Monica pulled Elsa to the classroom.

"You need to work your lazy butt." "My lazy butt. You think grandma is gonna keep," The next sound was Marcus slamming his foot down and a little wince like noise from Finn.

Inside the classroom, Ms. Shelley sat at her desk. The classroom filled fast as the bell rang. Finn and Marcus trampled over each other to get in. Elsa and Monica sat in the back. Elsa suddenly came to a realization.

"Hey." She whispered; Monica looked. "Did you actually work on the project at all?"

"No. My laptop got taken away until Black Friday. I have some of it written down but not a lot." Monica explained. "What about you?"

"I still have my laptop in my bag. Shouldn't be a problem." Elsa said.

Ms. Shelley stood up. "Now class. I received some emails about the projects. It is due on Halloween, no exceptions! She stated. "There's your shot to move your lazy butt." Finn whispered to Marcus. Marcus shook his head. "Use this class time to work on the project." Ms. Shelley looked over at Elsa and Monica. Hunter noticed.

"Aw Monster Monica and Eerie Elsa," Elsa had enough, she stood up and approached Hunter's desk, getting close enough for their noses to be only a few centimeters apart. Elsa fought the smell of Hunter's breath.

"Do I really need to lay you out again or has Hunter the Headless had his fill of dirt in his face?" Elsa retorted.

The class let out an "OOOOOOOO!" Hunter found himself without a comeback, he sat down defeated, mumbling "You're still a freak" under his breath.

The school let out halfway, some students rushed to the gym with decorations in hand. Elsa waited by the door for Monica. She knew her mom would be angry that she wasn't abiding by the terms of her grounding, although she wasn't sure if her mom knew it was a half day. Monica came sprinting out.

"You ready?"

"More than I'll ever be." Monica said.

"Great lets go."

"Just promise me one thing."

"What?" Elsa asked.

"I know you said we're heading to the cemetery. But we need to stay clear of the Caretaker. I really don't wanna deal with that jerk." Monica said. Elsa arched her eyebrow, but agreed nonetheless with, "Sure. Sure. Didn't know he existed, but yeah, we could avoid him. I guess." She mumbled the last part.

Reaching the cemetery seemed easier than getting to Jack's house, well in Elsa's head at least. She did worry about her mom catching her, but the building adrenaline rush in her system drove the thought out. It was an eerie feeling passing through the Iron Gate of Whipstaff Cemetery. Crypts lined the back horizon like pieces of a chessboard. But Keith and Allie's crypts were near the front line of graves. They looked like towers compared to the numerous crypts behind them. Monica kept an eye out for the Caretaker, no sign of him.

Elsa looked over to the gate, seeing some people pass by, but not enter. Calling out in a semi-whisper, "Jack?" Jack didn't answer.

"Jack?" Again, no answer. Elsa stepped forward, getting behind Keith's crypt.

"Jack!"

"Yeah!" Jack appeared behind the two, causing an "AHHH!" To come from Elsa. Elsa looked back at him; Monica turned. "Geez Elsa, you look like you've seen a ghost." Jack smiled, taking some joy in scaring Elsa.

"That's not funny." She said. "Really because you should see the look on your," Elsa punched Jack's shoulder, but her hand fazed through. "Nice." Jack said with a sly grin.

"How does that feel anyway?" Elsa asked. "To be honest, it's like pins and needles. You know like when a part of your limbs falls asleep." Jack explained. "And why the," "You get one of those punches." Jack quipped, knowing Elsa would ask. "Fazing I got no problem with." He added.

"Can you see him?" Elsa asked Monica.

"He's here?" Monica whispered.

"Take that as a no." Elsa looked back at Jack. "She would be," "Her name is Monica King. The other girl who went with me to your house." Elsa said. "Did not expect her to help, but ok." Jack said. The whispers from Jack's house pierced Elsa's ears and starting buzzing in her head once again. "Not again." Elsa held her hands against her forehead, but it didn't help. "Ah you're hearing the whispers." Jack said.

"You can hear them?" Elsa asked.

"What can he hear?" Monica interjected.

"Those whispers." Elsa confirmed. "Yeah, but I can never make out complete sentences." Jack said. "Yeah, those whispers are half the reason my side is bruised and slightly wrapped." Elsa said. "The stay away is the other half." She quipped.

"The what?" Monica asked.

"Didn't I mention that?" Elsa asked.

"That would be something that I would remember." Monica argued.

"Lucky you. Only words I've ever made out were queen and home, just a bunch of mumbling and rambling." Jack explained. This made Elsa wonder if the whispers were meant to be a message or just mumbling from the great beyond. "Well, I first heard them in your house." "Well, the fact you can see me and hear those whispers means you must be a medium."

"Monica said that same thing."

"What did I say?" Monica asked.

"The medium thing." Elsa confirmed.

"Oh. See I'm not the only one who thinks it. Thank you, Jack." Monica said, even though she couldn't see him. "You're welcome." He said, even though she couldn't hear him.

"Jack focus." Elsa said. "Right sorry." Jack said.

"Can I say something?" Monica asked. "Sure. Oh wait." Jack said. Elsa nodded. "If we're gonna help him. Maybe it be best to go where..." Monica hesitated, but she forced out the words, "He died." Elsa looked at Jack, he was rather uneasy.

"Lucky for you two, it's still standing." Jack said sarcastically. "Come on." He walked ahead. Elsa walked after him, Monica after her.

Past the headstones, behind the crypt, and deep in the forest, the trees were lush with green leaves that had yet to change color. The leaves crunched under Elsa and Monica's feet with every step they took. Monica felt the wind breeze through as she looked to the sky, the overcast hinted at an oncoming rain. A raven cawed nearby.

"CAW!"

"Where did that come from?" Monica asked, showing little sign of being scared.

"Not sure. But he does that a lot." Jack said.
"He's not sure." Elsa repeated. "I keep forgetting she can't hear me." Jack said. Walking through the forest, Elsa and Monica noticed the odd pattern of the trees. Some were tall, some were a few inches smaller. Some stumps rested nearby, some looked rotted, one looked freshly cut. Ahead of them was a circle of trees, the images on the trees catching Elsa and Monica's attention. Looking at the trees required a 360 turn.

"Whoa." Each of the trees had a different image carved into them.

A heart, A four-leaf clover, An Easter egg, A box of fireworks, A turkey, A Christmas tree, and a Jack-o-lantern. Elsa and Monica looked at each other, both amazed at how the images were carved and colored perfectly. Jack stood in between the Christmas and Jack-o-Lantern trees. He had a smile on his face. "Cool huh?" He asked. "Jack, you did this?" Elsa asked. "Yeah. Took me about three years." Jack confirmed. "What inspired you to do it?" Elsa asked. "I liked the trees in *The Nightmare before Christmas*." Jack said. "Come on." He walked ahead. Elsa watched as he fazed through the Halloween tree. She shook her head. She took three photos of the circle of trees then walked after Jack. Monica followed not so shortly after.

"It's just up here." Jack directed. "When you said by the cemetery, I didn't think you meant a hundred miles away from the cemetery." Elsa complained. "It's not that far. "Oh, watch out for the," Elsa tripped, and Monica tripped over her. "You two, ok?" Jack asked. "Yeah. Just fine." Elsa said, angrily. "I'm sorry. I keep forgetting about those branches. I faze through them. You can't." Jack said. "Yeah. Thanks for the tip." Elsa said sarcastically as she and Monica stood up. "Jack. Warn Elsa of anything next time, so she can warn me please." Monica quipped.

"Deal." Jack said.

"He agrees." Elsa repeated. "It's right up here." Jack took ten steps then he stopped. What lied in front of him forced the floodgates of his memories to reopen. His death now playing in his head like a broken record. The sight of the old church sent shivers up Jack's ghostly spine. The barking, the screaming, the rumbling, and the crashing of the stones falling in.

The old church was an old-fashioned brown stone building. The steps leading to the door were broken and chipped. Two of them looking rotted. One was almost unseen, covered with the tree vines that plagued the building from top to bottom. A circular window at the top, its glass window missing. Its frame broken beyond repair, the stone around it chipped away, it now rested by the door. The church's front doors were only half there. One door remained attached, the other lying on the inside. While the molding for the doors and the window looked non-existent.

The top of chimney on the left side of the church looked to have been hit with a wrecking ball but remained attached to the rest of the church.

He started breathing heavily, "I can't go in there." Jack turned around, but Elsa stopped him. "Whoa." Elsa said, she felt her hand touch the shoulder she tried to punch. She pushed him back a bit, then looked at Jack, confused. "Like I said, no problem with fazing." He said. "Ok. Listen," She grabbed his other shoulder. "No Elsa, I can't go in there!" "Why not?" She asked.

"What's wrong?" Monica asked.

"He can't go in there." Elsa said.

Why? Is there some spell barrier preventing him from going in?" She asked.

"Exactly like that, Monica. She's smart. Let's go." Jack tried to walk away. "Oh no you don't." Elsa stopped him. Monica couldn't see Jack, but she could sure see Elsa's arm go back and forth pushing Jack back. "Elsa."

"Jack!" "Look, just looking at this place makes me remember that I'm dead. That if I stayed home twenty-five years ago, all four of us would still be alive. Keith and Allie would be at some college far away. I would be the first person in my family to graduate from both High School and College. Nothing bad would've happened. I just can't go in there!" Jack explained, his eyes starting to tear.

Elsa started feeling bad for Jack, more than before. She watched as he wiped a tear off his face, his lips quivering. He went to sit down on a nearby stump, but fazed through, landing his butt to the dirt, and falling on his back. He angrily pounded the ground with his fist.

Monica noticed the look of concern on Elsa's face.

"It's not going well, is it?" She asked, concerned. "Elsa I'm sorry." Jack said, he didn't bother to look at her, preferring to keep his gaze to the sky. Elsa felt a chill down her spine, Monica shivered feeling the same chill. They looked at each other, then at Jack, at least Elsa looked at him. "Jack," Jack suddenly sat up and jerked his head towards the church. He rose to his feet so fast he nearly stumbled backwards. "What is it?" Jack looked at the church, the memories still flooding his head, but the call piercing his ears were too much to ignore. "Come on!" He ran into the church. "Well looks like he changed his mind." Elsa and Monica followed.

The interior of the church was chilly and slightly rotted. The stone walls were chipped, and the wood floor looked more rotted than the front door. Looking around the inside, Elsa and Monica noticed how the place didn't even look like a church. No pews, no religious portraits or statues on the walls, nothing in the place screamed church. "This was a church?" Elsa asked. "Looks more like a castle." She added. "Told you. It's one of the original buildings left from when the town started and abandoned as the town progressed with time." Monica explained. "Still doesn't look like a church." Elsa said. She looked up, tapping Monica's shoulder. They saw the hole where the roof had caved in, and the rubble where Jack was most likely crushed by the falling stone.

"Damn." Jack said. "What?" Elsa asked. "Something was calling my name. But it stopped." Jack noted. That's when he noticed Monica looking at the rubble. The memory of the roof caving in on him was like a disease in his mind. He stared at the pile, feeling his chest, remembering the pain from that night. He looked back at the caved in church, the stairs to the pipe organ broken from debris, the railing of the banister sticking out from rubble by the window, dried blood on it. He knew whose blood it was, Allie's screaming still in his ear. He remembered the sight of it, it was a nightmare he couldn't wake up from.

He walked outside, putting his hood over his head.

"CAW!"

"Oh, shut up." Jack mumbled to the crow. Elsa watched as Jack left; she saw him pull the hood close to the point where she could only see his nose.

Monica continued to stare at the rubble,

"Huh." She said. "What?" Elsa asked.

"Judging by the angle of this pile to the ceiling, this place couldn't have caved in." She explained. "What are you talking about?" Elsa asked.

"Well, if you stand right here." Monica positioned Elsa to a spot on the floor, then aimed her head at the ceiling. "See?" Monica asked.

"No." Elsa confirmed. "This rubble could not be from a regular cave in." Monica deduced. "A regular cave in?" Elsa asked, some sarcasm out like blood through stitches. "Elsa, this placed caved in no doubt. But not like everyone thinks." "Then how," "It didn't fall on its own, it was pushed in. Which means," Elsa realized where Monica was headed,

"Which means there was someone else here that night."

11

Shadows

Mayor Stine sat in his office, looking at his computer. The brightness of the screen played hell with his eyes. He leaned back in his chair, but relaxation wasn't an option.

"Excuse me Mayor Stine." Mayor Stine's assistant's voice echoed from the intercom.

"Yes Tim?" Mayor Stine asked.

"Vice Principal Myers is here, says,"

"Corbin? Send him in." Mayor Stine sat up as Vice Principal Myers walked in. "Corbin Myers. What do I owe the pleasure?" Mayor Stine asked. "Oh, come now Herman. What? No hello old friend." Myers quipped. "I've known you too long and I'm too tired for a pleasant greeting with you." Mayor Stine retorted. "The board's really breathing down your neck this year huh?" Myers asked. "That, I can't sleep, I'm going blind from looking at this screen, and to top it all off, the festival is tomorrow, and my wife keeps bringing up matching costumes." Mayor Stine explained. He sounded less than enthusiastic about the matching costumes.

"I hear you. Simpler times in our day; didn't have to worry about all this." Myers said. "Oh, I hear you. Sit down stay a while." Mayor Stine said, Myers sat down in one of the chairs in front of the desk. "So, I'll ask again, what do I owe the pleasure of this visit?" Mayor Stine asked. "Herman, I'm not one for this sort of thing. But,"

"Oh, come now Corbin spit it out." "It's been twenty-five years; I know we do the moment of silence every Halloween. But," "But what?" "I've been noticing certain things happening, the banner ripping in half.

102

Pumpkins smashed. A lot of posters with the word Halloween on them slashed. Even some decorations broken or full on destroyed,"
"All coincidences Corbin." Mayor Stine said, sounding confident.

"See I want to believe that. I really do. But lately I don't know." Myers explained. "Corbin. What exactly are you saying?" Mayor Stine asked, curious, but a bit skeptical. "Herman. This is going to sound weird. But I think Jack Harvey has risen from the grave and he's angry." Myers explained. "Jack Harvey?" Mayor Stine sat there in disbelief. "Yes." Myers confirmed.
"Why him?" Mayor Stine asked. "You know as well as I do. Keith and Allie were relentless with him from day one in middle school. No one ever helped that kid," "Corbin," "And we both know what happened in that church." Myers said sternly. Mayor Stine glared at him, "Corbin. Keith and Allie," "Wouldn't have been in there if it wasn't for Jack Harvey." Vice Principal Myers interrupted.

"Corbin, what happened that night was a freak accident. You know that, I know that." Mayor Stine explained. Like Corbin, he knew Keith and Allie just seemed hell-bent on tormenting Jack Harvey, but Mayor Stine didn't believe in Jack haunting anything let alone Keith's old teammates. Myers stood up, "Ok. Just wanted to let you know." "Corbin, I know you have a selective memory. Which is why I'm reminding you that this isn't the first time you've brought this up. Why do you keep bringing this up and, I'm not saying we are, but if we are being haunted, what makes you think it's Jack Harvey of all people?" Mayor Stine asked.

"I know I've brought this up before. My memory isn't that bad," "Well,"

"I know what you're going to say, and I'm done apologizing for that. It was a simple mistake." Myers argued. Mayor Stine chuckled. "No. No. Forgetting the victory party was happening is a simple mistake. Forgetting to book the venue and the caterers is not a mistake, it's something that nearly cost you your job. Had I not stepped in." Mayor Stein said with a touch of sternness at the end. Corbin sat back, annoyed. It had been mentioned to him before how much that "slip up" almost cost him and he was tired of hearing it.

"Anyway, I've said this before, and I want you to hear it this time. Even the nicest people can get pushed too far. You remember when Jack punched Keith. I think this kid has been lying in wait all these years. Waiting to come after every last one of us for never stopping Keith." Vice Principal Myers explained. Mayor Stine sat in his chair, his fingers tapping against his desk.
"Corbin. Yes, I remember when he punched Keith. But to be fair, Keith did threaten Harvey's dog if I recall correctly."

"I don't recall such a threat."
"Selective memory." Mayor Stein said. "Besides, it's been twenty-five years, a quarter of a century. If Jack was going to haunt us, he would've started from the day after he died as that list would be very long. Students and Teacher alike." He explained. "I get it though. The three of us. You, me, and Keith, we were like brothers. I miss him and Allie too. But Corbin, I want you to hear, listen, and remember. What happened that night was not Keith's fault, it wasn't Allie's fault, and it definitely wasn't Jack Harvey's fault. That old church was going to cave in eventually, they were in the wrong place at the wrong time. It shouldn't be that simple, but it is." Mayor Stein explained. Myers sat quietly, forcing his selective memory to retain that information.

"Besides, if we were ever to be haunted. It wouldn't come from Jack Harvey. It would come from Keith and Allie." Mayor Stine said sternly.

"Why them?" Myers asked, confused. "Keith would do it just to screw with us and Allie, well, you know as well as I do that, she never liked us that much." Mayor Stine explained. "She didn't care for Halloween either. Keith's getting an earful of that." Myers said. "May they rest in peace." Mayor Stine said. Myers sighed, "Corbin. Go home, get some rest because you look terrible if I'm being honest."

"You're right. You're right. I just get so worked up this time of year. I didn't mean to burden you." Myers said. "It's not a burden, I understand. But when you're fully rested and you get your head on straight again, give me a call, we'll go out to dinner and talk about the good old days." Myers smiled at that. "You got it. See you around Herman. I mean Mr. Mayor." Mayor Stine chuckled. "Take care Corbin." Vice Principal Myers walked out.

Mayor Stine leaned back in his chair, "All these years. He's still a character." The sound of scratching caught Stine's ears; it sounded like it was coming from his door. He briefly stood up, until he caught the sight of a tree branch grazing against his window. He shook his head. "I'm hearing things." Stine sat back down and leaned in his chair but leaned too far and fell backwards.

✳✳✳

Inside the cemetery, it was silent, some people walked the path to visit departed loved ones. The Caretaker was nowhere to be seen. A flock of crows flew into the nearest trees, not bothering to caw. The gray clouds covered the sun but showed no sign of rain. But all was not quiet nor was it peaceful.

Deep within a crypt, just near the front of the cemetery, lied a large coffin. Resting on a giant stone pillar slab, decorated with dead flowers. Mainly roses, some tulips, and a daisy or two. The coffin slowly opened, revealing a skeleton within. The skeleton's arms, decayed and fragile, were crossed in an X, covering the Steeple Hills cheerleading outfit. Two hands appeared out of thin hair, nails looked freshly done and painted hot pink.

"MY BEAUTY!"

The scream echoed through the crypt, cracking the stone door, and sending the crows into the sky.

12
Remember Me This Way!

Elsa and Monica sprinted to the library. Jack walked behind them, depressed. The place was empty, and the interior felt cooler than the outside. Five people occupied the table on the first floor. Monica recognized them as students from Ms. Shelley's class, no doubt trying to find material for the project, though one student just looked to be asleep, drooling over her notebook. Jack kept his hands in his pockets and his hood still up, though Elsa opened the hole before they left the cemetery.

Approaching the pumpkin-shaped desk, Elsa and Monica noticed Mrs. Prenderghast digging through the various newspapers inside. Frankie looked content in his cage; his can of food turned on its side. "Uh Mrs. Prenderghast?" Monica whispered. She turned around; her hearing matched that of a dog. "Oh, Monica dear. You're back already." She joked. "Hello Elsa, good to see you again." She added.

"Yeah, we're back." Elsa said. Mrs. Prenderghast suddenly shivered, "Oh that's strange. Did it just get colder in here?" She asked. "That might be my fault." Jack said. Elsa and Monica realized he was right. Elsa hadn't noticed it before, but whenever Jack was around inside, the temperature did drop. "Um, door draft." Monica lied.

"Mrs. Prenderghast. Can we speak with you in private?" Elsa asked. Mrs. Prenderghast squinted her eyes, at least that's how it looked through her glasses. "My dear, is this about Jack Harvey?" She whispered.
"Something like that." Jack said. Elsa looked back at Jack, "She can't hear you." She whispered.

"I take that as a yes." Mrs. Prenderghast said. "Go upstairs, I'll be up in a moment." Elsa and Monica nodded and walked past the desk. Jack followed, but Frankie let out a loud screech that caught everyone's attention.

"Hush Frankie!" Mrs. Prenderghast said, but Frankie wasn't listening. Jack just glared at Frankie then looked at Elsa and Monica, "Geez. Even when I'm dead he screeches at me." Then he walked up the stairs, briefly fazing through the seventh step before climbing back up. Elsa and Monica walked up the stairs, Monica got up fine. But the seventh step creaked under Elsa's foot, "Don't even think about it." She mumbled to the step, then she wondered why she was talking to a step.

The second floor was empty and, thanks to Jack's presence, cold. "I'll get the book." Monica said. She vanished into the stacks. "You really believe there was someone else there that night?" Jack asked, sitting in one of the chairs. "Monica thinks so." Elsa said. "But do you think so?" Jack asked. "I think that," Elsa hesitated. "She may have a point." Sh finished. Jack didn't seem so sure, he wondered if Elsa was being truthful.

"Got it." Monica returned, book in hand. Opening it the second time came without the old smell. "Ok." Mrs. Prenderghast arrived. "So, I would assume Jack is here with you." She added.

"Yes, he is." Elsa confirmed.

"Where exactly?" Mrs. Prenderghast asked. The chair Jack was sitting in slowly moved back, skidding the floor a little. Mrs. Prenderghast soon felt tapping on her shoulder. It felt like a chill running through her body. "Ok. So, he's,"

"Right in front of you." Elsa confirmed.

"How amazing." Mrs. Prenderghast reached out, almost as if to touch Jack's face. Her hand fazed through it, sending a pins and needles feeling through her hand. "My word." She said, astonished. Jack stepped back, rubbing his jaw.

"What's wrong?" Elsa asked, curious. "Pins and needles mixed with the stinging of Keith's punches. Sting a little more since her hand went into my teeth if I'm being honest." Jack explained.

"This is quite the week for you Elsa." Mrs. Prenderghast quipped. "You can say that again." Monica added, barely looking up from the book. "So. What is it that you would like to talk about?" Mrs. Prenderghast asked.

"We were wondering what you remember from the night of the tragedy." Elsa stated.

The astonishment on Mrs. Prenderghast's face faded away. It was like taking the light right out of her eyes. She adjusted her glasses, bringing them closer to her eyes. She went to sit in the chair Jack got up from, he pushed the chair to help her sit. Which still surprised her. Jack sat in the chair next to her.

Before she even said a word, that night flashed before her.

"It was Halloween night. I closed the library early because of the festival. I was handing out candy to the children on Main Street, right in front of Town Hall. It was beautiful, the festival was in full swing. Not a sad face among the crowd on the street. But that didn't last, we heard this rumbling, but we didn't give it a second thought. That was until someone had come running down the street and nearly tackled the sheriff. From what we heard later, Keith went to explore the old church with Allie, but never came back. The police raced to the church and found part of the roof had caved in, it took hours to get through the rubble. Allie's body was the first they found. Then Keith's. Jack was found last." Mrs. Prenderghast explained. The reflection of that night sent a morbid feeling throughout her body, her hands shook just thinking about the memory of the bodies as they were found. Jack placed his hand on top of Mrs. Prenderghast's, she instantly felt the pins and needle feeling.

"Did they find any other bodies? Like a dog's body?" Jack looked at Elsa confused.

"I told you I saw the prints in the dirt." Elsa held her hand up as if to calm him.

"No. No dog body." Mrs. Prenderghast confirmed. "Why would ask such a question?" She almost sounded offended.

"Jack says his dog Boris was in there that night. I just want to double check." Jack was sure that last part was directed at him. But Mrs. Prenderghast still nodded NO.

"Who ran to the sheriff?" Monica asked. Mrs. Prenderghast sat in silence for a moment or two, pondering the identity. "Oh, if anyone would remember that. It would be Sheriff Pullman." Mrs. Prenderghast said.

"Then I guess we're gonna have to go speak with him." Elsa suggested.

"Then let's go." Monica said, closing the book. "Mrs. Prenderghast," "Don't worry about it dear. I'll put it on your tab." She smiled. Monica smiled back and stuffed the book in her bag. "Thank you." "Thanks Mrs. P." Jack said, getting up from his chair, still neglecting that Mrs. Prenderghast couldn't hear him. "Thank you, from him too." Elsa said before she headed down the stairs.

Mrs. Prenderghast watched as the trio left the library, though she couldn't see Jack. The other people had already left, leaving the library vacant. But Mrs. Prenderghast still felt a coldness run through the place. She looked around, seeing no one. "I should've suggested a seance."

Frankie started to screech, startling her again. "Oh hush. If you remember correctly, I wasn't that bade at them. Though it has been a few years." She said. Frankie screeched louder flapping his wings, banging them against the cage.

"Prenderghast." A voice whispered.

"Hello?" Mrs. Prenderghast asked but received no answer. Frankie screeched louder, starting to bite against his cage.

"Prenderghast." The voice whispered again. "It can't be." Mrs. Prenderghast said.

"REMEMBER ME!"

Frankie watched in horror as Mrs. Prenderghast was attacked by an unseen force, it blew through the library like a tornado. Mrs. Prenderghast flew backwards, nearly hitting the staircase. Her attacker manifested itself in a dark purple glow in front of her eyes.

Mrs. Prenderghast looked up at her attacker, the face unforgettable. "I remember you." She said, her astonishment returning, mixing itself with her fright.

"GOOD!"

13

Creepy and Kooky

Sheriff Pullman sat at his desk. His hat on the rack behind him, his coat just below it. He scratched his head, believing he was feeling the thinning of his silver hair. The window was cracked open, the office was known to get stuffy rather quickly. Luckily, his screen was intact, the pitter-patter of leaves hit the screen as the window blew. A cup of cold coffee lied next to the sheriff's keyboard. He was looking at images of affordable housing in Florida. A knock caught his attention, "Yes?" He asked. A young cop poked his head in. "You busy Sheriff?" He asked. "What is it, Lloyd?" Sheriff Pullman asked. "Monica King and Elsa Carlyle want to speak with you." The mention of Monica's name caused Sheriff Pullman to roll his eyes. Monica had ridden in the back of his car more times than he can remember, but he never put her in the cells.

"Send her, wait. Both of them?" He asked. Lloyd shook his head. Sheriff Pullman was quite surprised. "Send them in." Sheriff Pullman ordered. Lloyd opened the door, letting the two girls walk in. Lloyd closed the door before Jack could fully enter, forcing Jack to faze himself through the door mid-closing. He shook off the pins and needles feeling.

"Usually when I arrest someone and let them off with a warning. I don't expect to see them in my office the next day." Sheriff Pullman quipped. "Yeah, this would make how many warnings for me?" Monica jokingly asked. "Seven." Sheriff Pullman replied coldly, rather quickly as well. "Sheriff Pullman, we need to ask you,"

"Just give me a moment please." He interrupted Elsa. He took a swig of his cold coffee, making a disgusted face. He pulled a bottle out of his bottom desk drawer. It was a tall white bottle with a spray top.

Duct-tape wrapped around it reading FLOOR CLEANER. He unscrewed the cap, pouring an orange liquid into his coffee. Monica and Elsa looked slightly disgusted; Sheriff Pullman quickly noticed. "Oh, don't worry. It's just Mel's pumpkin creamer." He whispered. "He gave three bottles last week; this is my last one." He explained.

"Why the floor cleaner label?" Elsa asked.

"I never got a drop out of the other two bottles. I changed the bottle and label to avoid anyone using it." Sheriff Pullman explained. He took another sip of his coffee, "Ah much better." "Oh, I'm sorry. Please forgive me. Where are my manners? Would you two like a drink?" He asked.

"We're good." Elsa said. Monica nodded in agreement. "Ok then." Sheriff Pullman put the cap back on the bottle and stuffed it back in the drawer. "Now to what do I owe this visit?" He asked.

"We want to know who came running to you the night of the tragedy." Elsa stated.

Sheriff Pullman looked at her, his right eye slightly twitching. "Now, Elsa, is it?" He asked.

"Yes sir." She confirmed.

"Why would you want to know that?" He asked. "It's for a school project." Monica interjected. "Really?" He asked, doubtful. "Yes." They confirmed simultaneously.

"It's for English class." Elsa said.

"But we want it to feel a bit realistic and to do that, we would just need a small piece of information from you about that night twenty-five years ago." Monica finished. Sheriff Pullman leaned back in his chair, sighing. He reached over and closed the window, but still felt a slight chill. He got up and closed his window. Elsa briefly looked back at Jack, who nodded. She smirked before turning back around. As Sheriff Pullman sat back in his chair, he looked at Monica and Elsa. "Please have a seat." Elsa and Monica sat in the wooden chairs in front of the desk, they were extremely uncomfortable. "It's hard to believe it's been twenty-five years. Still feels like yesterday. I still wish it's just a dream you can wake up from." He expressed.

"Three people die and,"

"Elsa. Let me ask you something. Have you ever watched someone grow up? Someone you see every day. Then in one tragic instant, see that," He paused for a moment, "That one life was snatched away." Sheriff Pullman asked. His words triggered a memory in Elsa's head, a memory of a time she wished she could go back and change.

"In a way I have." She said softly. "You never give it a second thought until it happens. It's traumatic and it leaves a deep scar. It's a nightmare that you wish you could wake up from and everything will be the way it was before. But then you pinch yourself and realize it's real." She added.

"Exactly. Especially when you realize there's nothing you can do about it. That old church should've come down long ago, would've prevented," Sheriff Pullman stopped, the memory of that night haunted him.

"Sheriff. We know someone came to you about it. Who was it?" Monica again interjected. Sheriff Pullman could tell she was determined to know the answer. Unlike Jack and Mrs. Prenderghast, the memory of that night did not flash before Sheriff Pullman.

"Back then I was just made sheriff. Little did I know that tragedy would be my first official job with the position. I remember back then that Keith Maitland was the star and captain of Gillman's basketball team." Jack shook his head and his air quotes.

"I think the only other player on that team that was as good as Keith was Herman Stine." Sheriff Pullman explained. "Mayor Stine?" Monica asked, shocked. "He's the one who told me about Keith exploring the church." Sheriff Pullman confessed.

"Wow." Monica said. "Well looks like we have another interview to do for our project. Thank you, Sheriff Pullman. Come on Elsa." Monica said. "Uh Monica." Sheriff Pullman called. "Yes?" Monica asked. "Stay out of trouble. I don't want to put you in the back of my car again." He advised. "I'll try." She said, sounding sweet as she stood up. Sheriff Pullman looked at Elsa. "Same goes for you Ms. Carlyle." He said as she stood up. "No promises." She said bluntly before walking out. Jack followed but had to faze through the door again.

Walking outside, the three of them noticed that night had fallen. The Halloween decorations lit up Main Street like fireworks lighting up the sky.

"No promises, really?" Monica asked.

"Oh please. Something tells me we're gonna end up in that backseat again." Elsa smirked.

"We are?" Monica asked, putting emphasis on WE.

"Why not? Could be fun." Elsa retained her smirk. Monica smirked thinking about it.

"Hey. Let me ask you something. What you said to Sheriff Pullman. Was that real or,"

"It was real." Elsa confirmed.

"What was it about?" Elsa hesitated before answering.

"I rather not talk about it." Elsa said bluntly.

"Understood." Monica said. She didn't want to push Elsa, not yet at least.

Jack stayed quiet, digging deep into his memory to try to remember anything about Herman Stine. Elsa looked at him, "You've been quiet. How much of a chord did that name strike with you?" She asked. "Honestly. I don't remember much about Herman. I barely interacted with anyone thanks to Keith and Allie. I'm not even sure what the guy looks like. Even if he is," Jack suddenly jerked his head. Elsa knew why.

"Calling your name?" She asked. "Yeah." Jack confirmed. "And it's louder this time. Gotta be close." Jack said. "Then go. We'll catch you tomorrow." Elsa said. "You got it. See you tomorrow!" Jack ran off, hoping this time he would find what was calling him.
"You hungry?" Monica asked.

"A little." Elsa said.
"You wanna grab a bite at Mel's? I think you'll love his pumpkin pancakes." Monica said.

"He serves breakfast for dinner?" Elsa asked.
"Oh yeah. All the time." Monica confirmed.

"Sounds like my," That's when Elsa felt a buzzing in her pocket. She pulled out her cellphone, seeing the word MOM dance on her screen. "Crap." She muttered before she answered. "Yeah mom?" Elsa rolled her eyes and held the phone away from her face as Wendy yelled at her from the other end. "Alright fine!" She hung up. "Problem?" Monica asked with an unintentional sarcastic tone.

"Yup. Gonna need a raincheck on those pumpkin pancakes." Elsa said.
"No problem. See you tomorrow?" Monica asked.

"First, do me a favor and put your number in. Can't do much if we can't use our laptops or not contact each other." Monica contained her excitement; Elsa was the first person to genuinely ask for Monica's number.

"Sure." Monica put in her number then handed the phone back. "Here." She said, fighting back a crazy smile. Elsa quickly typed in a message and Monica's phone vibrated with a text. "Now you got my number. I'll see you tomorrow. Wish me luck." Elsa said, then started walking away.

"Good luck." Monica said.

Jack ran down the street; the calling grew louder with every step he took. He found himself in front of the library. "Alright. Hopefully, I don't lose it this time." He ran to and through the library's front door. But the calling ceased, replaced with Frankie's sound barrier breaking screeching. The table was flipped, the chairs spread across the floor. Books thrown around, some ripped apart. Frankie's cage bitten open; it rolled a little on the floor like a melon on a lopsided table. "Mrs. Prenderghast?" Jack called, forgetting she couldn't hear him. "Oh. Dumb. Dumb Jack." He ran up the stairs, Frankie's screeching grew louder. He saw Frankie by the stairs, he looked down seeing Mrs. Prenderghast lying on the floor, unconscious. Her face pale white. Her glasses hanging from her neck, the right bifocal broken. "Mrs. Prenderghast?" He knelt down, feeling Mrs. Prenderghast's shoulders. He felt some warmth off of them. "Ok, still warm. You're not dead." He said with relief.

"Yet!" A raspy voice echoed. Jack looked around, seeing no one. "Hello?" He asked.

"HARVEY!" Mrs. Prenderghast's attacker charged in Jack's direction.

14

Who you gonna call?

Elsa walked through the front door, dreading what was about to happen. She took no more than two steps when,

"Kitchen!" Wendy called. Elsa turned, seeing her mother sitting at the table, not looking happy.

"Mom,"

"Where were you?" Wendy asked.

"I stayed after school a little to work on the project." Elsa lied.

"Really? Then why did I get a phone call from Sheriff Pullman that you and Monica paid him a visit?" Wendy asked. Elsa made a mental note in that moment, Sheriff Pullman wasn't gonna be an ally to her.

"Our project revolves around the tragedy in that old church. From what Mrs. Prenderghast told us,"

"Mrs. Prenderghast?" Wendy asked.

"Ok. We went to the public library yesterday after school. She says hi to you by the way. She mentioned that someone came running and screaming to the sheriff that night. We just wanted to know who it was. You know add some realism to the story." Elsa explained.

"Didn't I say it was here and school because,"

"Mom come on!" Elsa argued.

"No! You were grounded and," Wendy argued.

"How can I work on a project based on a specific event in a town I know nothing about if the only places I can go are here and school with a limited library and no outside communication?" Elsa argued, her voice getting a little loud. Wendy got up and stood in front of Elsa.

"Then you should have called me." Wendy argued.

"Like you would've listened." Elsa mumbled.

"Excuse me?"

"You never listen to me. I didn't want to move here in the first place but no, what I wanted meant nothing. Why did you even move me here in the first place?" Elsa asked.

"I wanted you to,"

"See that's it. You wanted. What about what I wanted for MY life mom huh?" Elsa argued.

"Ellie,"

"ELSA! FOR THE LAST FREAKING TIME, MY NAME IS ELSA!" She shouted. "YOU NEVER GAVE ME A REASON WHY WE MOVED HERE. YOU KEPT DODGING THE QUESTION!"

"I moved us here because of your grandparents,"

"Well, you're real late for that one mom. I barely remember them! All I have are the pictures you put away. Except for the one YOU put in my room! Maybe if you and dad weren't so stubborn, I would've known my grandparents more and actually cared more when they were GONE!" She shouted. Wendy remained silent, her anger growing. "Upstairs NOW!" She shouted. Elsa walked away without another word, halfway up the stairs, tears beginning to form in her eyes. Wendy watched as Elsa walked up and vanished into the hall, the slamming of her door echoing. Wendy covered her mouth, failing to fight back the tears in her eyes. She walked into the living room and glared at the mantel. She looked at the line of pictures. Her tears battling to escape her eyes.

But that's when Wendy replayed Elsa's words in her head. She looked at the very end of the picture line, seeing the picture of her mother and baby Elsa was missing.

"Wait!" Her eyes nearly popped out of her skull. "Holy crap. She ran upstairs, then down the hall, nearly colliding with Elsa's door. She pounded on the door until Elsa opened it.

"When did you see the picture in your room?" She asked.

"What?" Elsa asked.

"When?" Wendy asked again, her tone holding the potential of panic.

"This morning. I swear the way I felt it was like staring at me." Elsa said. Wendy's eyes shot daggers to her daughter. "What?" Elsa asked, not understanding.

"Kiddo. Answer me something. Do you see things that aren't really there?" Wendy asked.

"What do you mean?" Elsa asked, playing dumb as her mother's question caught her off guard, since they were just screaming at each other a minute before.

"Like…. Ghosts?" Wendy asked.

Elsa's eyes shot open. That was all Wendy needed.

"Oh my god." She said, stepping forward to hug Elsa tightly.

"Whoa mom." Elsa said, struggling under Wendy's grip.

"I had a feeling it skipped a generation." Wendy said, slightly crying.

"Wait say what now?" Elsa asked, shocked by her mother's words.

121

Monica sat at the counter inside Mel's diner, doodling in her notebook. The diner was a nice and cozy place to sit, eat, and study. Most of the booths were full and the small arcade area had a crowd forming. There were three games. Two of them were old school arcade cabinets, the third game was a pinball machine. The cabinet games were titled The Undertaking and Sonic Kong.

The pinball game was the Twilight Zone edition. "Ok." A near elderly man approached Monica with a large glass. "One pumpkin chocolate milkshake." The man placed it in front of Monica. "Thanks Mel." She said. "You want any whipped cream with it kid?" Mel asked. She looked at him, seeing Mel's smiling and semi-wrinkled face. His dark brown eyes equipped with his smile always brought a sense of charm to people who met him, made them feel welcomed. She smiled. "Maybe just a little." "Regular or pumpkin?" Mel asked. "I think you know." Monica joked. "You got it." Mel pulled out a bottle of pumpkin spray whip-cream from under the counter. There was a small fridge underneath for that and the creamers. He popped open the cap and sprayed some on top of the milkshake. "Thanks Mel." Monica said. "Anytime." Mel put the bottle back under the counter.

He noticed the crowd forming at the arcade. "You know. I should probably get more games over there shouldn't I? You know expand the arcade?" He asked. Monica looked over to the arcade. "Wouldn't hurt." She said. "But why are they crowding the pinball machine?" She asked. "Oh, they're watching Finn Deetz. He's been playing that game for about," Mel looked at his watch. "Three, yeah three and a half hours." He confirmed. "Three and a half hours?" Monica asked, surprised. "Yeah, came in with Marcus. Ordered a pumpkin peanut butter milkshake, got some quarters, and started playing. Although, I think he's still using his first quarter, maybe his second. Either way he should be close to the high score by now. He got close last week." Mel said. "What happened?" Monica asked. "Hunter tilted the machine." Mel said. Monica shook her head. "Yeah, I know." Mel said. He understood Hunter was a jerk. "Anyway. You want anything else?" He asked. "I think I'm ok with the milkshake right now." Monica said. "No problem. If you change your mind let me know. Enjoy." Mel said. "Thanks." Monica said, continuing to draw and write some parts of her project as she took a large slug of her milkshake, leaving her with a small milk mustache.

Monica's purple pencil rolled towards her notebook, soon rising. Monica's eyes shot open as the pencil began writing on the page in front of her.

MIND YOUR BUSINESS…. OR ELSE!

The pencil stayed in the air. Monica wondered if Jack was playing with her, she couldn't see or hear him. So, in her head, it was possible Jack was messing around. "Very funny Jack." She whispered.

The purple pencil wrote… NOT JACK IDIOT!

AC

The pencil's tip snapped off; then looked to snap itself in half. The paper soon slashed itself in half. Monica soon felt a cold shiver as the pencil fell to the paper, like something ran a finger up her spine.

"HIGH SCORE!" Marcus called out, startling Monica. She yelped a little, but it was drowned out by the cheering crowd.

Elsa sat on the edge of her bed, Wendy standing in front of her. Elsa was shocked silent, Wendy nervously rubbed her hands together, occasionally cracking her knuckles.

"So, let me get this straight. This ability to see ghosts runs in our family?" Elsa asked.

"In a way yes. Your grandmother told me a long time ago that it started for her when she was an adolescent and that it goes back to our ancestors. I'm talking the generations before my great grandmother's grandmother." Wendy explained.

"But yet, it skipped you." Elsa noted. Wendy sat next to Elsa. "Yes, it did. I never understood why. My mother first told me about it when I was ten. So, I figured it would come with puberty. But it never did." Wendy explained.

"And it just started for grandma?" Elsa asked.

"According to her, yes." Wendy said.

"And this is why,"

"The fact I didn't have the ability caused a rift between your grandmother and I." Wendy explained. "I guess in a way, not having it made me feel like some kind of outcast in my own home. But back then, I didn't realize that I wasn't the true outcast. My mother was." She added. "All those years of arguing, I should've seen the truth. I was just too stubborn. That's another thing that runs in our family, from both sides." Wendy chuckled a little, but it didn't make her feel any better. All the years of arguments swam in her head like an Olympic swimmer.

"So, I guess me having it brings back that whole outcast feeling for you huh?" Elsa asked.

"A little. But this time I'll get over it." Wendy said.

"Mom, I'm," Wendy hugged Elsa tightly before she could finish her sentence, again trapping Elsa's arms under her grip.

"It's ok." She said softly. "What hurt most is that I said basically the same thing to my mother when I was your age." Wendy said. "Although if you say it again, then we're gonna have an issue." This got a small laugh out of Elsa. Wendy loosened her grip.

"Do you hear that?" Wendy asked, the sound of tapping catching her ears. Elsa looked at her large window. She knew exactly what was causing the tapping. She opened the curtains and opened the window. "Get in here." She said. Jack walked in. "You know, you can faze through the window, right? Or do ghosts suddenly need permission?" Elsa said sarcastically.

"First off, that would be a vampire. Second, I lied earlier, I do have trouble fazing through certain things. Wood and metal fine, glass, and anything fluffy, not easy for me for some reason." Jack explained. Elsa noticed Jack had this panicked look on his face.

"You, ok?" She asked.

"I got all the way to the library. But when I got inside. It wasn't pretty." Jack said, but that's when he caught sight of Wendy. "Oh, I'm sorry am I interrupting?"

"No. What,"

"Wait. I remember her." Jack said.

"What?" Elsa asked.

"Wendy Walker." Jack looked back at Elsa. "You never told me Wendy Walker was your mom." "You never asked." Elsa sarcastically quipped. "Wait how," "She was a senior when I was a junior." Jack explained. "She was really cool in High School. Actually, a lot of guys thought she was,"

"Please don't finish that sentence." Elsa stopped him, a bit embarrassed and slightly sickened. "What happened at the library?" She asked.

"The place got turned upside down. That bat bit out of his cage. I got upstairs and Mrs. Prenderghast was knocked out on the floor." "Wait what?" Elsa asked.

"Mrs. Prenderghast got attacked!" Jack basically repeated. "Is she ok?" Elsa asked.

"She should be. Before I left, I set off the library's alarm." Jack said.

"What would that do?" Elsa asked.

"Should get the medics and police there." Jack said. "Um kiddo?" Wendy exclaimed, suddenly feeling like the C in an A to B conversation. "Oh right, what we just talked about. Yeah, there's a ghost right in front of me so," "Really? Who is it?" Wendy asked, doing her best to hide her surprise of a ghost in the house. "Mom. Does the name Jack Harvey ring any bells?" Elsa asked. It did.

"Jack Harvey? Yeah, it does. He was one of the victims in the cemetery tragedy twenty-five years ago." Wendy said, standing up. "Good. I mean not good. Never mind. What I mean is, Jack Harvey is here." Elsa explained. "Like right here." She gestured to where Jack is standing. Wendy's eyes shot open. "You're serious?" She asked. Elsa looked at Jack. Jack knew what he had to do to convince Wendy of his presence. "You feel the slight chill?" Elsa asked. "A little?" Wendy said, slightly skeptical. She was always skeptical of her mother's ability to see ghosts, even more when she didn't develop it. But now that she knew Elsa harbored the ability, Wendy's skepticism began to die down a little.

"Long time Wendy. Pardon me please." Jack lightly touched Wendy's shoulder. She felt it. Elsa could tell by her mother looking at her shoulder.

"Pins and needles feeling?" Elsa asked. "Yeah." Wendy confirmed with slight fear in her voice. Elsa was relieved that Wendy now fully believed her.
"Ok. Jack, what attacked Mrs. Prenderghast?" "Mrs. Prenderghast?" Wendy interjected. "Yeah. Jack says she was attacked not too long after we left." Elsa explained. "Wait you said you went to the library yesterday?" Wendy noted. "Yesterday and today actually." Elsa said almost sheepishly, realizing she had lied about going today. "We'll talk about that later. Anyway, what attacked her?" Wendy asked.

"About that. This is gonna sound weird." Jack said. Elsa shot him a look. "Poor choice of words, sorry. What attacked her, attacked me too. I know exactly who it was." Jack said.
"Who?" Elsa asked. "It was Allie." Jack confirmed. "Allie?" Elsa asked. "I thought you said," "I know what I said. Twenty-five years walking through the whole cemetery and all of Steeple Hills, never once was there any instance of either Keith or Allie returning as ghosts. But all of a sudden, here's Allie attacking me in the library." Jack ranted.
"You're sure it was her?" Elsa asked. Wendy stood there silently, letting Elsa speak with Jack, though it just looked like Elsa was talking to herself.

"Oh, I'm sure. It didn't look like Allie. Looked more like, have you ever seen *Ghostbusters*?" Jack asked. "Yeah?" Elsa asked, skeptical. "Well, it looked like the librarian ghost at the beginning. You know all purple and see through. It definitely wasn't Allie's face, but the Steeple Hills cheerleading outfit and her voice was a dead giveaway." Jack explained. He re-thought his words. "No pun intended." He added. "She wore her cheerleading outfit on Halloween?" Elsa asked.

"Oh, I remember that. Allie Crane was so vain she would wear the cheerleading outfit day and night for the rest of her life if she was given the chance." Wendy interjected.

"She couldn't be righter." Jack said. "I firmly believe she became evil when she put the outfit on." He quipped.

"So, she was buried in it?" Elsa asked. Wendy nodded. "We were buried in what we were found in. This," Jack pointed to his hoodie and jeans, while pulling his hood down. "If you haven't figured it out yet, this is what I was wearing that night. Ok they didn't put these clothes on my corpse just so I would be comfy while I was six feet under." Jack ranted. "Allie was buried in her cheerleading outfit; Keith was buried in his costume." He added. "Which was?" Jack had to think for a moment. "He was dressed as *Beetlejuice* but without the crazy hair." He remembered. "Though his letterman jacket was draped over his body, I saw that in the coffin."

"That's, kinda wrong." Elsa noted. "We weren't even given proper wakes funerals. Well, I wasn't. I just got thrown into the ground. Cheap coffin, short goodbyes." Jack said. "Keith and Allie were given nice luxurious cushy coffins; I don't fully understand that. I mean it's not like the bodies are gonna toss and turn in there. Plus, you saw their crypts. Though I'll admit that their parents shelling out a lot of money for the coffins and crypts, but not really spending a dime to put their kids in proper death attire, never made sense to me." Jack noted, though he believed he may have overthought it. Elsa just nodded. "All I know is, I saw our bodies in the morgue. All of our parents." He paused.

"Well, my parents, actually just my dad. He couldn't even look at my corpse." Jack said.

"What is he saying?" Wendy asked. "Mom. How long of a time period was there between the tragedy and the burials?" Elsa asked. Wendy closed her right eye; it was a sign she was in deep thought, something neither Elsa nor her father understood. "I say about two maybe three days." She said, though she wasn't completely sure.

Jack squinted his eyes in thought, trying to remember when he first woke up as a ghost. "Thaaat sounds about right." He said. "Everyone expected wakes and funerals, but nothing happened." Wendy explained. "It kinda surprised everyone that the Cranes and Maitlands didn't do anything." She added.

"That's some bull-" A sudden boom like noise stopped Elsa. She walked over to the window. "What the?" She asked rather loudly. Wendy and Jack approached the window.

Down below on the lawn lied a message, one engulfed in flames.

STAY AWAY!

"Ok. Even for Allie, this is taking things way too far." Jack said. "That's it. I don't care if I have to call the *Ghostbusters* or the freaking *Exorcist*, we're taking this bit-" The ringing of Elsa's cellphone cut her off. She saw it was Monica. "Monica what's up? What? You, ok? Hold on," Elsa held the phone to her shoulder, then looked at Jack. "After Allie attacked you what happened?" She asked. "Nothing. She knocked me down the stairs and when I looked up, she was gone. Why?" Jack asked. "Because the bitch just threatened Monica at Mel's Diner with the same damn message." Elsa said, fuming. Jack stood there, he was more surprised than shocked, but a little bit of horrification crept onto his face. Wendy was just as horrified.

15
Mean, Mean, Mean

Arriving at Gillman the next day, Elsa struggled to keep a low profile, especially with Jack next to her. It had been another night for Elsa without sleep, though Elsa fought it off instead of sleep evading her.

She was also struggling to contain her anger at Allie's threats. Deep breaths and constantly clenching and relaxing her fist didn't help. Elsa wasn't too far from the school door when she heard Jack utter, "Dang!" "What?" She asked. "I don't know who that was that just walked through me, but that dude has got some major BO." Jack complained. "Come on." Elsa said, chuckling a little. Monica waited on the other side of the door, a little shaken up from her encounter in Mel's Diner.

Nothing much scared Monica but having a personal encounter with a threating spirit that she couldn't see, did put cracks in that wall. She tapped Elsa's shoulder as she passed. Elsa stopped and looked at her. "You good?" She asked. "I will be." Monica said. "You?" She asked. Elsa looked over her shoulder then back at Monica. "We'll be good. But there is something I need to tell you." Elsa whispered everything from last night into Monica's ear. She stepped back, awaiting Monica's reaction. "It runs in your FAM," Elsa covered Monica's mouth. "Seriously?" She asked. "Sorry." Monica said, muffled by Elsa's hand. "Let's go." Elsa removed her hand.

Elsa and Monica walked into the main hallway, Jack behind them. Several students in the hall were dressed up for Halloween. Students dressed as various characters spanning across from classic monsters like *Dracula*, cartoons like *Space Ghost* or *Scooby Doo* Fred and Daphne couple costumes. One girl was dressed as *Scary Godmother* and one boy was dressed all in black. Long black pants that stopped at his ankles, a black button-down shirt, and black thin framed glasses with his black hair combed backwards. He walked around with a smirk on his face. Monica and Elsa looked at him as he walked past them. "Who is he supposed to be?" "Looks like R.L. Stine from the *Goosebumps* movie." Monica said. "I've only seen that movie on someone else's TV, but I can see that." Jack agreed. "I can't believe its Halloween already." He added. "Yeah, time sure flies, don't it?" Elsa quipped as she glanced at Jack. "Was that a jab at," "Uh-huh." Elsa confirmed. "Slightly deserved that." Jack said.

"Any update on Mrs. Prenderghast? I didn't hear much from my police radio." Monica asked. "I visited her in the hospital last night, she looked fine to me and are we going to ignore the fact Monica has a police radio?" Jack said. "Got it. Jack says she looked fine to him." Elsa repeated. "Apparently we are." Jack noted the ignoring. "Ok, how do we deal with," Monica was cut off by her bumping into Marcus.

He turned around, his wore the mask of Barrel from *The Nightmare before Christmas*. "You know first she bumps into Finn and now you bump into me." Marcus joked. "Oh, that was bad." Finn said, appearing almost like out of nowhere, his costume that of some realistic scars painted on the left his face, mostly stemming from his jaw line to the corner of his mouth. "Hey Finn." Monica said. "Hey. How you two doing?" Finn asked. "We're good. What happened to your costume? Heard you were going as John Constantine for Halloween?" Monica asked. Finn nodded his head, Marcus started to snicker. "He was. But his creativity got the better of him."

Elsa's eyebrow shot up, "And that means?" She asked. "The sleep walking dead over here tried to hook up a small gas hose around his arm to his hand and managed to not only singe himself, but also managed to burn half his costume to ash. So instead of Constantine, he looks more like Jonah Hex." Marcus explained. Finn didn't like that comment and the look he shot Marcus showed it.

"I thought you had an aversion to fire?" Monica asked. "I was, uh, willing to put up with it for the sake of the costume." Finn said.

"Well at least you tried to be creative." Elsa said. She looked over at Marcus, "But yet all he has is a mask, which doesn't seem to be covering much." she quipped. It rendered Marcus silent. "Nice one." Jack said. Finn just shook his head and laughed a bit. "So, Finn, how you doing after your victory?" Monica joked.

"Victory?" Elsa asked. "Oh, last night at Mel's, Finn got the high score on the Twilight Zone pinball machine." Monica explained.

"Thank you, Monica, for making me sound like I really have no life." Finn said sarcastically. "You know, Monica ain't wrong cuz. No offense. See you guys in class." Marcus walked into Ms. Shelley's classroom. Finn knew Marcus was just being Marcus, a grade A pain in Finn's rear end.

"Ouch." Elsa said. "Jokes on him. My name's the only one on the project." Finn smirked then walked into the classroom. "I know I'm the last one to talk, but they're weird." Jack stated.

133

In the classroom, Ms. Shelley herself stood with her back to the class, scribbling Happy Halloween on the board. She turned to face her students, revealing her costume. She was dressed as Winifred Sanderson from *Hocus Pocus*, the only thing missing was a red wig. Elsa and Monica sat in the back, their desks side by side. "Happy Halloween!" She announced.

Looking over her class, Ms. Shelley saw all the costumes they wore. It was a mix of various costumes, Frankenstein, Dracula, Jack Skellington, Homer Simpson, even one girl had a Marge Simpson costume on, tall blue hair included. "Now as most of you have probably already heard. Our dear public librarian, Mrs. Prenderghast, had a bit of a spill in the library last night. From what I've heard, she's going to be just fine, and I believe will still be in attendance for the festival later tonight." Ms. Shelley explained.

"Word travels fast." Elsa noted in a whisper. "Small town, fast press." Monica quipped in a whisper. "I guess us getting arrested didn't travel that fast." Elsa mumbled. "Yeah. Normally it doesn't because it's me. But you being involved, It should've." Monica added.

"You sure Jack will be ok walking around the school? I mean, I know no one else can see him but," "How much harm can he do by exploring the hallway? But if we hear someone scream, then we get him." Elsa said. "Sounds good to me." Monica said. They both knew it wasn't the best plan, but they went with it anyway.

Hunter entered the classroom. His clothing looked torn, his face looked pale, and his lips and teeth looked to have a little smear of red lipstick on them. "Hunter, so nice of you to join us. Let me guess. Your costume is someone who was in a rush to get to school." Ms. Shelley joked in a cheesy fashion.

"What cos- oh right! I'm half asleep. But I'm a Werewolf victim."
Hunter's tone of voice matched his half-asleep exterior.
"You believe that?" Elsa asked. "The half-asleep part yeah. But the
costume, not so much." Monica said. She never tried to give Hunter a
second thought, but she couldn't shake the feeling something else was
going on with him.
"I pray your project is just as creative as your costume." Ms. Shelley
quipped.

"Now Mon," Ms. Shelley fell silent for a moment. "Monica. No
costume? At the risk of sounding sarcastic, I'm intriguingly surprised."
She said. "Oh but Ms. Shelley I am in a costume. I'm a homicidal maniac
they look just like everyone else." Monica smirked and looked at the
class. They laughed, assuming Monica was joking.
But when Monica dropped her smirked, they fell silent and turned
around to avoid looking at her, though Finn and Marcus each gave her a
thumbs up. Ms. Shelley looked only slightly amused; she looked over to
Elsa. "And Elsa, shall I ask what your costume is?"

"Simply a master of fright, and a demon of light." Elsa smirked
and leaned back a little in her seat, despite the chair being unable to
move. None of the other students would look at her. Ms. Shelley
appeared to scan Monica and Elsa with her eyes. "I see you two are
going to be quite the pair." She said, turning her back to the class,
approaching her computer.

"Now, we'll be watching a film in celebration of Halloween. But
before we do, please hand in your projects. Come get some candy while
you're at it." Several students approached Ms. Shelley's desk. Some
projects were thin, little of them were thick. Monica and Elsa did not

leave their seats. Over the course of the last few days, neither one of them had managed to finish the project.

"Is that everyone?" Ms. Shelley asked. Monica looked at Elsa, winked, and then got up from her seat. "Sorry Ms. Shelley couldn't find it at first." Monica plopped a fifteen-page project onto Ms. Shelley's desk, taking two pieces of candy from her basket. She sat back down; Hunter didn't say a word as she passed. He was uncharacteristically quiet. Monica took her seat before she tossed Elsa a chocolate candy. "You finished it?" Elsa whispered. "Don't worry about it." Monica winked. She popped the candy into her mouth. Elsa smirked, her fondness for Monica growing as she popped the candy into her mouth. "Now, for our feature presentation." Ms. Shelley clicked play.

"When you've been around as long as I have man." The film's narrator started; it had a Jamaican accent.
"Oh. Wait, sorry. Not that one. That's for my grandchildren tonight." Ms. Shelley stopped the film.

"Ah yes. Here's the one." She clicked play. Whimsical music echoed as the film's title displayed itself on screen in big orange lettering. It was followed by the narration,

"One of the first things you learn in life is that things aren't always the way they appear to be."

Jack wandered through the hallway. For most of his afterlife, Jack avoided the High School, at least the inside of it. He hated the idea of going to the place when he was alive, with thanks given to Keith and Allie. But now in death, and with Elsa and Monica's help, the urge to explore was too strong.

Wandering the halls of Gillman, Jack gazed at the beige lockers and white plaster walls. "All these years later and nothing's changed." He realized. A corkboard full of papers for play auditions, music lessons, part-time job opportunities, college prep course sign-up sheets, and a sign-up list for PSAT study classes, hung in the hallway, just as Jack remembered. His encounter with Allie stirred up his memories like stirring up milk to bring the chocolate powder to the top.
In life, he had failed at his best to avoid her. But in death, Jack was overcome with a sense of heart beating wonder, if only his heart was still beating. He turned a corner and walked past a set of lockers, but stopped in his tracks as he gazed at his old locker.

The number on it read 1408.

Jack looked at the locker, glancing down at the lock. He spun it to 19, then to 8, then 6. It clicked open. He didn't bother to look around to see if anyone saw a locker open by itself. The locker was empty, but to Jack, it was fuller than it should've been. His life flashed in front of him,

25 Years Ago:

Keith slammed the locker shut, jamming Jack's fingers inside. "OW! Seriously?" Jack asked.

"Saw you ran out of Science, trying to avoid me, Jack?" Keith snarled. His hazel eyes shot daggers at Jack, who tried to avoid eye contact. "Look at me!" Keith forced Jack to meet his gaze. "Is little Jackie Harvey scared?" Keith mocked.
"I told you to stop calling me that."
"Little Jackie Harvey!" Keith sang mockingly.
"Enough Keith."

"Oh Keithy, you're not having fun without me, are you?" Allie appeared out of nowhere. She batted her brown eyes at Keith, twirling her long hair. "Oh of course not baby, just getting little Jackie warmed up." "Goodie." Allie mocked.

"Don't you two have somewhere else to be? Like the gym so you can actually get good at, AW!" Jack was cut off, and winded, when Keith nailed a hard punch to his stomach. Jack slunk to the floor, Keith yanked the locker open, setting Jack's fingers free.

"Little Jackie Harvey!" Allie sang. Keith knelt down, casting a shadow over Jack. "You listen to me; this is only going to get worse for you. Don't think because we're graduating that our fun with you ends. Now stand up you're embarrassing yourself." Keith said angrily. Jack struggled to stand up, which annoyed Keith and Allie. "Keithy, he's taking too long." Allie complained, then nailed a swift kick to Jack's stomach. "AW!" Jack yelled in pain.

"Nice kick babe." Keith said, impressed. "Thank you. I figured I break in my new pointed shoes." Allie boasted. "Very nice. But I'm sure you can kick higher." Keith flirted. "Don't be fresh Keithy." Allie said; she knew exactly why Keith wanted to see another kick.

Jack forced himself to his feet, "About time." Keith said. He pushed Jack against the locker, "This will never end," The bell rang, and the student body began swarming the hallway. "See you around Jack." Keith playfully slapped Jack's face. He put his arm around Allie and started walking away. But Keith couldn't help himself. He walked back to Jack, who sounded like he was coughing up a lung, "See you in gym," He launched his fist into Jack's stomach, the pain felt like 1000 bee stings. The sound that escaped Jack's lips was a mix of a cough and a scream of pain. The next thing Jack saw was a bit of blood on the linoleum floor.

Present:

Jack snapped out of his trance and closed the locker. His stomach began to hurt, the feeling of those painful kicks returned with a vengeance. He rolled up his hoodie and the green t-shirt under it. He looked at this stomach, seeing the large bruise Keith and Allie left on him that day. "What the hell? How?" He looked back at the locker, panic on his face. "This was a mistake. A huge mistake." He said softly, his breathing getting harder. He covered his stomach and backed away from his old locker. He could hear the taunting song in his head, playing like a bad record.

"Little Jackie Harvey, Little Jackie Harvey, Little Jackie Harvey!"

He covered his ears, but the song still echoed.

"Little Jackie Harvey, Little Jackie Harvey, Little Jackie Harvey!"

The locker doors began to shake as the song echoed. Jack uncovered his ears, "This isn't in my head." He realized. Jack followed the song, it continued to get louder with every step Jack took. Despite his encounter, he was certain it wasn't Allie singing. Jack stopped, finding himself in front of the gym as the air went silent. "Oh, come on." He complained. The smell of the boy's locker room below wafted from the staircase. Jack waved the smell away from his nose, "Oh man. Twenty-five years later and that locker room still smells worse than a dead body."

The school's trophy cases lined up behind Jack. Various trophies filled the shelves, most of them championships for baseball and football. There were few trophies for basketball. Jack counted them all, coming out with ten. He noticed that the trophies for basketball had stopped his freshman year and didn't start again until the year his class graduated. Up above the trophies hung various pictures, each one no bigger than 24x32. A total of seven frames lined the wall. These frames were the school's wall of fame, their way of honoring coaches or athletes that had made an impact in the school's history but died too young. Out of the seven portraits, only four of them were former students. None of them were portraits of Keith or Allie. But looking down the hall sent Jack back into his trance.

25 Years Ago:

Jack walked out of the locker room; the smell nearly made him vomit. The bell rang and Jack bolted up the stairs, he ran across the gym. But a basketball smacked into the side of his head, leaving a ringing in his ear. "Little Jackie Harvey! Little Jackie Harvey!" Keith's singsong made the ringing in Jack's ear feel worse. "Not trying to outrun me are you, Jack? We both know you can't do that." Keith mocked. "I'm almost insulted that you would try. Almost insulted to the point where, maybe, just maybe, teepeeing your house isn't enough. Maybe egging it might do the trick." Keith said. It didn't take long for the rest of the gym class to see what Keith was doing.

"I mean, your house looks like crap anyway. Egging might make it look better. Hell, breaking a window or two might help. Oh, but don't worry, I'll leave you some candy. Some for your parents. Why not, some for that ugly mutt of yours. How about a nice king-sized chocolate bar!" Keith mocked, then started laughing.

Jack's eyes filled with rage, he felt his fist clench, all he saw was red. The next thing he heard was a loud OOOOOOOOOOOO and a thud. When the red died down, Jack saw Keith lying on the ground covering his bleeding nose. "KEITHY!" Allie screamed as she ran to him. Jack looked at this hand, blood stained his knuckles.

"Oh crap." Jack said, realizing what he had done. The other students looked at him, but most looked at the Keith, who looked to be furious. Jack didn't know what to do, but his legs did. He clutched his bag tightly and bolted out of the gym like his feet were on fire. The ending bell rang as Jack left a little bit of smoke in his wake outside the school's front door.

Present:

Jack snapped out of his trance as the bell rang, sending the students scrambling around the hall.
He walked away from the trophy cases, having had enough of seeing the year he had lost. As he took one last look at the cases, he felt that pinch in his chest. Running his hand over his sweatshirt covered torso, the pinch seemed to fade. The pinch had been happening for years, but Jack

never understood it. "Again?" He looked to the glass of the first trophy case, being a ghost, Jack had no reflection. But the sudden appearance of Ali's face sure made it look like he did. "AH!" Allie's appearance in the glass spooked Jack backwards. But when he looked again, Allie's face was gone. Jack turned to leave, but bumped into the gym coach, who looked a bit wrinkly.

"Whoa kid. What's your hurry? Better move slow or you'll trip over your feet going too fast." The coach said, his voice hoarse as if he had smoked an entire pack of cigarettes. He limped as he walked past Jack. This confused Jack.

"Coach Carson?" The coach turned, already halfway into the gym. "You can see me?" Jack asked.

"Well sure Harvey, am I not supposed to see you?" The coach asked. Jack didn't have a response. "You looking a bit pale kid. Go get yourself checked by Nurse Davis." The coach walked into the gym, leaving Jack alone in the hallway. Though he wasn't really alone, none of the few students walking in the hall could see him.

"Nurse Davis? She retired my junior year." Jack said to himself, before he looked at the gym. "How can he see me?" Jack asked.

He took a brief glance at the wall of fame before looking back at the gym in confusion. But then a thought came to his head, he looked back at the wall of fame. "Wait." He saw one of the portraits hanging above the trophies. The black hair, the hint of a mustache, the football quarterback build. It all matched. The portraits plaque read...

Coach Timothy Carson
May 26, 1965 - February 14, 2010

A breeze blew through, shaking the portraits from side to side. Coach Carson's portrait fell off its hook, landing face first onto the trophy case. Jack stood there silent, fright and confusion mixing throughout his head. "Hey kid." Coach Carson called. He looked back at the gym, Coach Carson still standing in the doorway. But now he looked identical to his picture. The smile he had on his face wasn't a pleasant one. It was a twisted smile, the kind that would make even the toughest of people squirm a little.
He pointed at Jack, "She's coming to get you!" He warned, a chilling singsong tune in his voice. The lights began to flicker, Jack looked up at them. The two bulbs flickered like the ticking of a clock.

"Little Jackie Harvey! Little Jackie Harvey! Hi Jack. It's been too long."

16
The Dead Shall Be Raised

Elsa was grateful Gillman made Halloween a half day for school. Even more grateful she didn't have to attend Math. Monica walked out of her history class, meeting Elsa in the hallway. "Ok so, town hall, talk to the mayor?" Elsa asked. Monica's attention was caught by a man in a blue collared shirt and tan pants walking past them. "Maybe not. Come on." Monica walked forward, "What is it?" Elsa asked. Monica looked back at her, "The mayor is here." Monica kept walking until she caught up with Mayor Stine.

"Excuse me Mayor Stine." She said. He turned to look at her.

"Yes?" He asked.

"Monica King reporter for the Gillman Gazette, any chance my partner and I can interview you for the school paper?" Monica asked.

"Why yes of course." Mayor Stine confirmed with a smile. Monica pulled out her notebook,

"Question one, are you seeking reelection in next year?" Monica asked.

"I'm considering it yes." Mayor Stine confirmed.

"Question two, any big plans for the Halloween festival tonight?" Monica asked.

"Actually yes, this year we've added Pumpkin Painting as part of the festival's arts and crafts and also we've added a screening of *The Nightmare Before Christmas* to be projected on the side of the old theater, figured it be fun for the theater's last hurrah before demolition." Mayor Stine said.

"That does sound fun and a great way to honor the theater. Question three, how do you plan to honor the victims of the tragedy since this year marks the twenty-fifth anniversary?" Monica asked.

"Well, that's a very good question. Every year we have a moment of silence, and this year will be no different. I've had a special tribute made to honor my old classmates for this special anniversary." Mayor Stine said.

"Great. Next question, feel free to stop me if this rings too personal. What was your connection to the three victims?" Monica asked.

"Oh, don't worry. You see, Keith Maitland and I, actually, along with vice principal Corbin Myers, we were all on the same basketball team back in High School, all three of us were friends since we were about ten years old, like brothers to be honest. But Ms. King, I must say that's my only connection. I never had the chance to really get to know Allie Crane well and, truth be told, I never really spoke to Jack Harvey, but I remember hearing he was a nice kid." Mayor Stine stated.

"Ok. Now final question, again, stop me if it's too personal. What were you doing on that night?" Monica asked. Elsa felt that might've pushed it, especially after seeing Mayor Stine appear to stiffen up.

"Well Ms. King, the team was attending a Halloween party that night, I was just discussing it with Vice Principal Myers. That's about it." Monica wrote down all the answers in her notebook then ripped out the paper.

"Hold this for me." She handed it to Elsa. "Mayor Stine, we thank you for your time." Monica said.

"It was my pleasure Ms. King, Happy Halloween." Mayor Stine walked away, Monica and Elsa watched as he exited the school. Elsa looked back at Monica, "Impressive." She said. "Thank you. Now the

Vice Principal. Chuck that." Monica walked ahead. Elsa crumpled the paper and tossed it in the trash can. Walking down the hall, the student costumes seemed to get darker and, some, more mature than there should be for a high school. Monica looked around at the students that passed, they had all heard of her and the nickname Hunter had stuck her with. They treated her as if she was infected with some kind of disease.

They looked at Elsa the same way. But at this point, all that could be said was "Halloween has clearly stopped being a kid's holiday." Elsa noted. "Yup. Teens and adults have ruined it for generations to come. Office is over here." Monica said. The brisk breeze hit the two as they walked into the office, it was clear this time to Elsa that a window was left open.

Mrs. Strode remained at her desk, wearing a Sarah Sanderson costume, her blonde hair prevented the need for the costume's wig.

"Monica King. What can I do for you today?" She asked, not taking her eyes off her computer screen. She sounded less than pleased to see Monica.

"We need to speak with Vice Principal Myers." Monica said. "We?" Mrs. Strode looked away from her keyboard, seeing Elsa. "Forgive me. You've come in here alone so many times, I never expected anyone else with you. Especially the new girl." She said, though Elsa didn't appreciate the implication or the snob like attitude. "Anyway, yes, he's in his office. Please knock first, he's been on the phone with the superintendent all day." Mrs. Strode asked.

"What for?" Monica asked.

"Discussing budgets and other stuff students don't need to know about." Mrs. Strode said coldly, returning her gaze to her computer screen.

"Come on." Monica walked ahead. Elsa shot Mrs. Strode a look, keeping the gaze as she followed Monica. Mrs. Strode looked over her shoulder as Elsa walked ahead, feeling a shiver down her spine. Monica knocked on Vice Principal Myers' door.

"It's open." Monica opened the door.

"Ms. King, it's been a while. Do come in." He said. "Oh, my apologies." He said, catching sight of Elsa.

"Ah, Ms. Carlyle correct?" He asked.

"That's correct." Elsa confirmed.

"Ah, and the mayor thinks my memory is shotty. What can I do for you two?" He asked. Vice Principal Myers wore a button down light blue shirt with black pants. Monica sat down in one of the chairs in front of the desk. Elsa chose to stand.

"Vice Principal Myers. We actually just spoke with Mayor Stine,"

"Oh Herman. Yeah, him and I were just reminiscing of our days here as students." Vice Principal Myers said.

"That's always fun." Monica said. "Anyway, we'd like to talk with you about the tragedy." Monica explained. Vice Principal Myers leaned back in his chair with a perplexed look on his face.

"Oh. Wow. No student has asked me about that night before. Hard to believe it's been twenty-five years. But what would you like to know?" He wondered.

"We just want to know what you remember." Elsa said.

"Oh, quite simple. Keith and Allie came to my house that night. We were supposed to go to this Halloween party that was being thrown by one of our teammates. Keith and Allie weren't actually invited, but they were notorious to show up at parties anyway. They loved to crash parties." Myers chuckled. "But that night, before we left. Keith did tell me that he and Allie were going to check out the old church. Between us, I believe he was going after Jack Harvey. He loved to torment that poor kid." Myers explained.

"Why is that exactly?" Monica asked.

"To be honest with you Monica, I truly have no idea. Maybe it was because Keith was popular, Jack wasn't. Keith's family was wealthy, Jack's wasn't. I asked Keith a number of times, but he never really gave me an answer. One time I asked, he just looked at me and laughed. But that day I had some sort of a reason for the torment, but it was only for that day. I always had a feeling that Jack would eventually snap and fight back. That day I was proven right. Jack had finally fought back and punched Keith. Anyway, I warned him not to go. I didn't trust that place, no one in town did. Everyone knew it would eventually cave in. But Keith was stubborn at times. He said they would be late to the party. But when neither he nor Allie showed up, I ran to the old church. That's when I found them. All three of them. I'll spare you two the gruesome details."

"Oh, don't worry. We can handle it." Elsa assured, though she sounded sarcastic.

"No. What I saw that night. I rather not burden you with it. I will admit that while I'm not prone to hyperventilating, I did find it hard to breath when I saw them. When I," He paused. "Composed myself. That's when I ran to the sheriff. I couldn't sleep well for months after that. The whole basketball team was put on grievance therapy for a few weeks after that." Myers explained.

"Did their opinion of Keith change after that?" Elsa asked.

"A little. You know never speak ill of the dead. But the rest of the basketball season, we started winning the games again. But there were times the team believed we were cursed. Mainly when we struggled in the first half of most games. Sometimes, the second half. You know karma and all that. Some of the team members spoke ill of Keith behind his back when he was alive, my attempts at defense were futile. But they still blamed Keith whenever we started losing." Myers explained.

He rubbed his hand over his mouth, his fingers grazing the stubble he had around his jaw. "Not a day goes by that I don't miss Keith. I mean how could anyone not miss their best friend." Myer said, his eyes getting misty. Monica looked at Elsa, she returned the look. "Vice Principal Myers. The reason we're asking is because," "We think that there was someone else there that night. Someone who pushed the stone to cave in the roof." Monica interjected. Myers looked at the two girls.

"Excuse me?" He asked, sounding a bit offended. "We went to the old church. The way the stones looked; it didn't just fall. It was definitely pushed. We spoke to the sheriff and," Monica explained. Myers wiped the mist away from his eyes.

"Monica." He interrupted. "I can't believe you would come up with such a disrespectful idea." He stood up. "Of all the students here, I never thought you would speak so ill of the dead. Considering your mother and father." That struck a chord with Monica. A very tight chord that forced her silent. "Now get out!" Elsa stared at Vice Principal Myers.

"Listen,"

"No Ms. Carlyle, I have lived with the memories of that night for the last twenty-five years. This town has lived with them. All of sudden you move in and disrespect our past. Not in my office. I'll say it again, get out!" Elsa grabbed Monica's arm and left the office. Myers slammed the door shut behind them. "Why are new students always a problem." He mumbled.

Elsa led Monica out of the main office. "Have a nice day." Mrs. Strode said, coldly. Elsa stopped and glared at her. Mrs. Strode quickly looked away. Elsa almost pushed Monica out the door.

"Come on." Monica said. "Hang on." "No hang on." "Monica!" Monica didn't stop, "Hey!" Elsa grabbed her shoulder to turn her around. Elsa now saw that Monica's eyes were mistier than Vice Principal Myers' were.

"What did he mean by considering your parents?" "It's nothing." Monica tried to turn away, but Elsa stopped her. "Hey. Start talking." Monica relented. "Fine. I don't live with my parents. I live in a foster home. Ok." Monica explained.
"My parents didn't want me! They dropped me on the foster home's doorstep and bolted out of town! They might as well be dead now!" Monica's eyes got mistier.

Elsa knew the feeling of only having one parent. But not having both parents because they didn't want the child. That was something else. Monica rested her head on Elsa's shoulder, nearly crying into it. Elsa didn't bother to push her off, she wrapped her arm around Monica. "It's alright." She whispered.

In the back of her head Elsa was formulating a plan for revenge on Vice Principal Myers, while another part of her brain was coming to the realization that she was caring for Monica as a friend.

"Wait." Monica stepped back, interrupting Elsa's inner thinking. "The Sheriff." "Wow you comeback fast." Elsa noted. "You listened. That's all I needed. But anyway, Sheriff Pullman said Mayor Stine came running. But Myers said he ran to him,"

"EELLSSAA!"

Jack's voice echoed through the halls; several lockers burst open as if hit by a strong force from the inside. Elsa and Monica looked at each other, then ran down the hallway.

Finn and Marcus walked back inside. The sound of the lockers was loud enough to be heard from the courtyard. "Um, that wasn't because of you, was it?" Finn asked. Marcus had to think about it. "I don't think so. But if it was," Finn and Marcus looked at each other, their eyes shooting open as if it was a secret code between them. They nodded, then walked out the door rather quickly.

Elsa and Monica stopped at the gym; the hallway was empty. The glass of the trophy cases was cracked, like someone had punched them. The portraits of the wall of fame were tilted, two of them were tossed around the floor like they were hit by a tornado. No sight of Jack. "JACK?" Elsa called out. "JACK?" Monica copied. She didn't care that she couldn't hear Jack, she knew he could hear her.

"Hehe." Elsa turned to the gym. Coach Carson was standing there, the twisted grin looked permanent. He stood there, with a hunch, flipping a coin. "It's too late for little Jack Harvey." He said. His voice near demonic.

"Who are you?" Elsa asked. Coach Carson didn't answer. He let his coin drop to the floor as he decomposed, his clothing and skin faded away leaving his old bones to hit the floor, becoming dust upon contact. Monica looked, not seeing Coach Carson. "I'm guessing it's not Allie?" She asked. "No. It's a gym coach." Elsa noted. "As in Coach Carson?" "Who?" Elsa asked. She turned around, seeing Monica holding one of the portraits.

Monica turned it around, showing the coach's face. "This Coach Carson. He was struck by lightning years ago." Monica explained. "And he was just walking around." An idea popped into Elsa's head, a horrifying Idea. "Monica." "What?" "You being the expert, answer me this. What's the word for raising the dead?" Elsa asked. "Necromancy." Monica confirmed. "Why?" She asked, though subconsciously she knew the answer. "Oh, I think you know why." Elsa quipped. "Allie took Jack and,"

"LADIES!" Elsa turned seeing a woman sitting in a wheelchair, wearing a police uniform, just missing the belt and her right. Gray hair down to her shoulders. "Get to class!" She ordered.
"Oh, don't listen to her." Elsa turned the other way, seeing another man, dressed in full suit and tie. He was missing the back of his head. "She's just angry since her leg didn't grow back in death. Complained about it the whole travel here." He explained. "Annoyed the lot of us." He added.

"There's more of you?" Elsa asked, though she regretted it. "Elsa. How many more are there?" Monica asked. "Right now, I see two."
"Excuse me." Elsa looked over to the gym, where Coach Carson once stood, now stood a young woman with scars on her face and arms. Her

brown hair and pink dress dripping water. "I think you mean three."
Some water escaped her mouth as she spoke. Elsa looked at Monica.

"Allie took Jack, and she's raising the dead."

17

Good Ghouls Gone Bad

Elsa led Monica upstairs into her room, both near running.
"Nice room." Monica said. "Thank you. Ok so what do we know so far?"
Elsa asked, replaying every event from the day she arrived in Steeple
Hills in her head.

"Ok, so you moved here, met Jack Harvey. Then you found out he's a
ghost still walking around town from a tragedy twenty-five years ago
that killed him and his two bullies. He has no idea why he didn't
crossover, but yet one of his bullies turns up from beyond the grave,
attacks Mrs. Prenderghast, and captures Jack in our High School while
also raising the dead for…. reasons unknown, all while you find out
seeing ghosts runs in your family. Did I leave anything out?" Monica
asked, she spoke rather fast. Elsa looked at her, "No that's pretty much
everything." She confirmed.

"Obviously, Allie would take Jack because of their past, but why
raise the dead?" Monica asked, Allie's reasoning eluding her. Elsa's door
opened and Wendy walked in.
"Hey. I thought we agreed you would keep your door," That's when she
caught sight of Monica. "Oh hello. Am I interrupting?" Wendy asked
with slight sarcasm. "Actually, you might be some help. Mom this is
Monica. Monica, my mom."

"So, you're the famous Monica my daughter's been talking
about." Wendy said.
"I guess so. You have a lovely home." Monica said, partially flattered
Elsa mentioned her to her mom.

"Why thank you. It was my parent's house actually." "Ok since the whole introduction portion is over, let's get down to business." Elsa interrupted. "What business?" Wendy asked, crossing her arms. "Well. Here's an update. You remember Jack Harvey, the ghost I can see thanks to the power bestowed upon my blood from Grandma."

"I remember." Wendy confirmed.

"And you remember how he discovered recently that Allie is back too,"

"Our lawn remembers that too." Wendy retorted, looking angry while doing so.

"Well, Allie has taken Jack. As well as started to raise other spirits from their resting place." Elsa explained rather quickly.

Wendy stood there confused. "Ok, I just have one, maybe two questions."

"Shoot." Elsa said. "Why would Allie take Jack?" She asked. "Or raise the dead?" She added. "Those." Elsa said. "Are excellent questions as to which we don't have the answers yet." She added.

"We think Allie took Jack because of their past." Monica explained.

"So, it's possible that Allie believes that Jack could be responsible for their deaths?" Wendy asked. Elsa and Monica looked at each other, the idea never came to their heads. They both nodded, mentally agreeing that was possible. Wendy smirked, but she hid it. "But raising the," Elsa stopped. A noise catching her ear. Even through the closed windows, the noise was loud.

"Elsa?" Monica asked. "What is it kiddo?" Wendy asked. "Do you hear that?" Elsa asked. "Hear what?" Wendy asked. "The whispers again?" Monica asked. "Yeah." Elsa confirmed. "They're getting louder." She added, almost sounded like she was proud. She walked over to the large window; she threw open the curtains. The trees moved apart just like they did on Elsa's first night, giving her a look at Main Street. She saw people gather on the street and an idea came to her head. "Wait!" She looked back at Monica and Wendy. "Jack said Allie was vain. That she would wear her cheerleading uniform all the time if given the chance." She explained. "Which means what?" Monica asked. "She's a diva. Always was." Wendy stated. "Yes. But it would also mean that if she's gonna make her presence known now that she's back," "She's gonna do it in a spectacular fashion!" Monica finished. "Now answer me this, where is the best place to do it tonight?" Elsa asked. Wendy and Monica quickly realized, with horror building in their eyes. Wendy was the first to say,

"The Festival!"

18

Spectracular

Down on Main Street, the festival was in full swing. Hundreds of people in costumes. Mayor Stine stood at a podium, his costume that of Raggedy Andy. His wife stood by him, her costumes that of Raggedy Ann.

"Good evening, everyone!" He announced. "Now before we get started, I must announce that our town librarian Carrigan Prenderghast could not be in attendance tonight due to a little spill she had yesterday. But I've spoken with her, she's doing just fine and will be back in the library by the weekend. She wanted me to wish everyone a Happy Halloween tonight. So, enjoy yourselves, have fun, and most importantly HAPPY HALLOWEEN!" He shouted with glee.

"Also, before I stop talking, I have something very important to do. This very night twenty-Five years ago, Steeple Hills was dealt with a horrific event, a tragedy that took the lives of Keith Maitland, Allie Crane, and Jack Harvey. So, my old teammates and I have put together this tribute to show that twenty-five years later that night will never be forgotten, and those poor souls will always be remembered and honored. We initially wanted to do this at the old theater, but Stoker's Grocery Store has a much better-looking wall." Mayor Stine said, though the last part sounded like a poor joke. He stepped down from the podium, allowing the projector to illuminate the side of Stoker's Grocery store. It started with the words.

IN MEMORIAM

People started to tear up watching the film's montage of clips featuring Keith and Allie, there was no clips of Jack. Keith's yearbook photo came on screen. It soon faded, letting Allie's picture appear. But before Allie's picture could fade, the screen froze. The technician started pounding at the keyboard, confused by the freezing. Elsa and Monica ran to Main Street. They got to the tribute just as Allie's face breached the projection. Emerging from the screen like a zombie from its grave. The wall cracked as she fully appeared.

Her scream echoed like a force of nature, blowing the iron gates of Whipstaff Cemetery open and off their hinges. Gravestones cracked and crypt doors burst open. Spirits emerged from the cemetery. They flooded the streets, but they stopped before touching Silberling.

The townspeople ran in terror as the ghosts raided the festival. Finn and Marcus found themselves in the middle of the chaos as spirits chased the townspeople. "Dude?" Finn asked, looking at Marcus. "I swear, this isn't me." Marcus argued. Two ghosts flew into them, laughing while they did it, sending Finn and Marcus into the air, flipping over the pumpkin painting table as well. Allie hovered above the chaos; it amused her. She grunted and pointed towards the cemetery.

Sheriff Pullman sat at his desk, contemplating busting out his "floor cleaner" in his desk. But the ringing of his phone broke his desire for the "cleaner".
"Sheriff. Excuse me? Is this a joke? Yeah, yeah, Happy Halloween." He hung up. "Ghosts on Main Street, ridiculous."
"I know right." The Sheriff looked ahead of his desk, seeing the ghost of Sheriff Elfman, a man who was Sheriff thirty years before the Sheriff

was born, sitting in one of the chairs. "It's so ridiculous." He said. The Sheriff's eyes shot open, he let out a loud "AHHHHHHHHHHH!"

Outside on Main Street, the ghosts began pushing the crowd of people towards the cemetery as Allie vanished. Mayor Stein at the front of the crowd. Wendy joined Elsa and Monica on Main Street, horrified at the chaotic scene. "Mom, please tell me you can you see any of this." Elsa said. "Oh, I can see it." Wendy confirmed. "Allie must have emitted some sort of spell to allow this." Monica said, though she wasn't exactly sure. "We'll figure that out later." Wendy said. The ghosts looked to be doing more than just scaring the people of Steeple Hills, they were pushing them into formation like teachers lining up their students. "Where are they leading them?" Wendy asked. "I think there's only one place Allie would want everyone to see her really return to the land of the living." Monica deduced. "The place where she died." Elsa realized. "A delusional dead cheerleader with a goddess complex. How original." She added.

Inside the church, the ghosts pushed the townspeople inside. Elsa, Monica, and Wendy ran after them. The screams of the townspeople filled the old church, Mayor Stine was thrown to the center of the room.
"Hello everybody!" When people looked, no one could see who was talking. "Up here!" At the top of the stairs, Allie stood with her hands on her hips. Her fingers tapping away impatiently as if she was waiting for a single spotlight to shine on her. Her cheerleading uniform looked exactly as it did when she died, with blood on her skirt and shoulders and some on her face, which looked scarred. Her legs scraped; her heels

broken open at the tips. Though her arms looked untouched, her elbows were blood red. She flipped her long dark hair as she descended the stairs, as if she was a queen without a royal guard to carry her. In Jack's Day, she would have an evil smile on her face, but she wasn't smiling now.

"Twenty-five years. TWENTY-FIVE YEARS!" She started to glow a pink-ish color, "YOU DID THIS TO US!" She hollered.

"Us?" "Who's us?" Some townspeople asked. Allie rolled her eyes in annoyance.

"Fine." Allie looked at the top of the stairs and snapped her fingers. Two spirits, clad in 1950 black leather jackets appeared at the spot where Allie stood before. They looked like extras from *Grease*, inverted elephant trunk hairstyle and all. Allie gave them a thumbs down. The two spirits responded by pulling Jack from the floor and tossing him down the stairs. Allie got joy by watching him roll down the stairs and crash to the bottom.

"The nobody formerly known as Jack Harvey everybody!" Allie half-heartedly announced.

Jack stood up, holding the back of his head, and rubbing his neck.

"Formerly?" Jack asked. "Didn't know you knew that word." He added.

"Yeah well, you were a nobody when you were alive. Somethings never change." Allie said, ignoring Jack's remark.

"Now. For those of you who don't remember. I mean let's face it, you've all forgotten about me, allow me to explain anyway." Jack rolled his eyes, knowing Allie would look for any reason to talk. "Twenty-Five Years ago, my beloved Keithy and I, and that poor lump of space over there," Jack shook his head, even in death Allie was a pain.

"We were in this church on Halloween night. But the roof caved in and well here I am today. A freaking ghost. While my body, my beautiful body, is reduced to nothing more than a horrific skeleton, which now is nothing but a pile of dust. I mean it seriously discolored my uniform."

"Not like the blood on her shoulder didn't do that already." Elsa mumbled. Allie shot her a look,
"Excuse me little Ms. Nobody. Allie is talking." Elsa arched her eyebrow, not fond of Allie's comment and her eyes showed it. She was starting to both understand and share Jack's dislike of Allie a lot more. "Now. Like I said, here I am, a ghost. Be sure to thank my murderer," Jack cleared his throat as if to remind Allie he was involved. She rolled her eyes. "Fine. OUR murderer. Do you always have to ruin my moment?" Jack just shook his head, silently wishing Allie would just disappear. "Anyway, that man would be Mayor Herman Stine!"

The townspeople gasped in shock. Mayor Stine got to his knees, befuddled at the accusation. Even Jack was shocked.
"What? I didn't kill you. I wouldn't. Why would I? I wasn't anywhere near, Allie you're not making sense." He pleaded.
"Not like she ever did." Jack announced.

"Shut it!" She bellowed at Jack, then returned her attention to Stein. "I know it was you!"
"Allie please listen, you know this isn't right. I never would've hurt you or Keith. Sure, you and I weren't close, but Keith was like my brother. Why would I kill him?" Mayor Stine asked. He finally stood up; Corbin Myers stepped behind him, clad in black cowboy costume. He pulled off the hat and fake mustache so he could speak.
"Allie he's right. Keith was our teammate, our captain."

"Yes, we should've stopped him back then. You remember how stubborn he was. We should've put up a bigger fight with him." Some tears formed in Mayor Stine's eyes. "We've missed you two every day since. Please let these spirits rest and let the townspeople go, they've done nothing but honor you since that day." Mayor Stine pleaded. Allie looked over to Jack. He held up his hands, showing he wanted no part of Allie's afterlife revenge. Allie looked back at the ghosts.

"NO!" Allie's scream sent a wave of wind through the church, causing some stones to break away and crash into the stairs. Jack flinched a bit, remembering his death. "Oh please, it barely touched you." Allie complained.
"Allie," "NO! This wasn't part of the plan. My plan was to make you SUFFER!" She screamed. More stone from the roof began to fall. The crowd began to scream, "Oh relax you bunch of," Allie looked over at Elsa and Monica. "YOU TWO!"
"I knew you looked familiar. I warned you to stay away and to leave this alone." Elsa stepped forward.

"So, you WERE the one who sent me through the floorboards and burned the message in my lawn." She said. Though she knew full well it was all Allie, Elsa wanted to hear it from Allie's mouth. "And the one who haunted me in the diner." Monica added.
"And I thought blondes were the dumb ones." Allie said in a condescending manner. "But clearly neither one of you listen." She added.

"Yeah, you see. I have this problem with being told what to do." Elsa was missing her sunglasses and Allie got a look at the anger dwelling in Elsa's eyes, like a dragon lurking in a deep cave. Monica stepped forward, "And I have a real problem with being threatened."

"You just couldn't mind your business." A small growl like grunt echoed, but no one could see where it came from. Allie waved it off as she raised her hands, beginning to ascend into the air.

But Elsa grabbed her left arm and yanked her down to the ground. Allie struggled to fully stand for a bit before she composed herself and stood shocked, "What? How did you?"

"I was able to see Jack Harvey before anyone else. You really think I can't take you down."
Allie squinted her eyes, "What kind of freak are you?" Before Allie could do anything, Elsa nailed her in her scarred ghostly face with a hard-right punch. Wendy's eyes shot open, Monica smirked, Jack's eyes shot open, Mayor Stine and Vice Principal Myers didn't know what to do. But the spirits and townspeople let out a loud OOOOOOOOOO, while some were amazed Elsa made contact.
"That hurt! Why did that hurt? I thought that couldn't happen." Allie complained, rubbing her face. "You are so lucky I'm not alive. You could've broken my nose. Me getting hit was not supposed to happen!"

"Well now you know how I felt." Allie looked back at Jack, he knew she had the punch coming, after so many years.
"By the way. You wanna know the truth. It wasn't,"
"Girls!" Corbin Myers interrupted Monica. "Everyone. Please let me ask. Allie, it's been twenty-five years. We all knew this place was going to cave in one day. I hate to even say this but, does it really matter that much anymore? I mean after all these years; it doesn't matter that Keith was pummeling Jack in here before the roof caved in. Doesn't matter,"
"Hold up!" Jack called, everyone looked at him as he made his way to the center of the room. Allie took a step back, though she didn't like losing the center.

"Yes Mr. Harvey?" Mayor Stine asked.

"Corbin. How did you know that?" He asked. Corbin stared at him, puzzled.

"What?"

"He asked you; how did you know that." Elsa stepped next to Jack, Monica on Jack's other side. "The only way you would've known about that was if," Jack stopped.

"What?" Allie asked, starting to sound a little angry.

"It was you!" Elsa announced. "You pushed the stones in!" Jack stated. Mayor Stine looked at Corbin Myers. "Corbin?"

Corbin looked over to Jack, then back at Stine. "Please, this kid's nuts. He's doing this to cover his tracks. We all know that he hated Keith. He probably goaded Keith into coming in here, rigged the stone to fall and kill him. You wanted to end Keith's torment so bad you kill him to do so!" Vice Principal Myers stated.

Jack's anger breached the surface, "THAT'S NOT TRUE!" He yelled. His outburst sent a shockwave through the church, nearly bringing down the rest of the second floor. It was like a volcano exploding after many years of being dormant.

"Whoa!" Monica said, surprised. The townspeople flinched in terror. Jack didn't care at the moment if they were growing scared of him. But Allie took two steps back. Jack never scared her before, that moment was a first. Even from looking at him from the side, she could how he really felt. His eyes full of anger and hate.

"It's not true! I didn't kill him!" Jack argued, Elsa put her arm out in front of Jack. Mayor Stine looked at Jack, Corbin's words echoed in his head, "Even the nicest people can get pushed too far." He said aloud.

"Well, I didn't do it." Corbin argued. "Keith was my friend, my teammate. You were his victim for years and yet you dare accuse me of killing him. Just because you pushed him out of the way when the stones fell doesn't make you a saint Jack!" Jack's anger refused to subside, even with Elsa's arm blocking him. Though he contemplated walking through her arm in that moment.

"Now how did you know that?" Elsa asked, fighting the urge to smirk.

"Know what?" Myers asked, looking at Elsa.

"How did you know Jack pushed Keith out of the way?" Monica asked.

"Well Corbin?" Wendy stepped next to Elsa. Mayor Stine and Allie looked at Corbin. He stared ahead at Elsa and Monica.

Despite Jack and Allie's presence, the room suddenly felt hot as if the flames of hell had invaded the room. He didn't want to ask the question for he feared the answer. But Mayor Stine knew he had no other choice.

"Corbin. What did you do?"

Corbin Myers looked at Mayor Stine, sweat pooling on his panicked face. His breathing got heavy as if an anvil had been pressed against his chest.

"It was an accident." He confessed. The townspeople gasped, though Elsa felt it was a bit overdramatic. "How could you?" Allie asked.

"You said he was your friend." Jack said.

"Oh please. Keith was no one's friend. He had an ego he didn't deserve. He worked for nothing, he had everything handed to him. All because he was dating this brat." Corbin looked at Allie, a scowl on his face. "Our coach didn't care about talent and the whole team knew Keith didn't have it. He didn't care Keith was the cause of our losing streak. He only cared about making his spoiled niece happy. Pulling strings to make you head cheerleader and Keith the captain of our team. Both squads suffered because of the two of YOU!" He nearly hollered.

"But I never meant to kill him. I just wanted to scare him. I didn't even mean to push the stones. I saw Keith from the hole. I saw you two drag Jack in here. I leaned forward trying to get the right angle, but the stone slid out from under me. Even when he tortured you for so long, you pushed him out of the way. Very honorable Jack." Corbin said, mockery in his voice. Allie was speechless.

"When I realized what happened,"

"You pushed the other stones in, forcing the roof to come down and you ran off to lie to the sheriff." Elsa finished. Corbin glared Elsa, the look in his eyes was that of an unhinged animal.

"And I got away with it for twenty-five years. That was until you showed up and started digging." He said.

"Actually, it was you who told us." Monica interjected. "When you told us earlier that you were the one who ran to Sheriff Pullman," "But when we spoke with him yesterday, he said it was Mayor Stine who told him about Keith and Allie." Elsa added.

"You see, here's how that night really went down. You went after Keith because you knew what he was going to do to Jack as revenge for Jack punching earlier that day." Monica stated. "You figured scaring Keith would help you somehow. Perhaps delusionally believing that Keith would be so traumatized that he almost died from this place, that he would quit the team and you can start winning." Elsa added.

"We figured since you mentioned seeing the bodies before anyone else. It gave you the right amount of time to run to Stine and lie to him about the cave in," Monica explained. "All in order for you to cover your tracks." Elsa finished. Myers stood there in shock, feeling a loss of breath for a moment.

"Looks like karma's finally caught up with you Myers." Jack argued.

"Oh, please Jack. That crap didn't help you then, it's not gonna help you now!"

"That's what you think!" Sheriff Pullman, with Sheriff Elfman behind him, quickly slapped a pair of cuffs on Corbin's wrists.

"Hold on!" Jack called. He lowered Elsa's arm, giving her a look that mentally spoke "Trust me." He walked up to Corbin. "Even the nicest people can get pushed too far." Mayor Stine repeated.

"I agree." In that one moment, Jack felt the same feeling he felt the day he finally gave Keith what he had coming and nailed a punch straight to Myers' face.

Sheriff Pullman looked over to Allie, who stood silently in shock.

He took her silence as a NO to hit Corbin, who shot Elsa and Monica a dirty look as he was escorted outside. Sheriff Pullman started reciting the Miranda rights, while Corbin tried to shake off the sting of the punch. "I know my rights!" He angrily announced.

"Good, then you remember the right to remain silent!" Sheriff Pullman retorted. Sheriff Elfman looked to the other ghosts, "Come on. Back to sleep with the rest of you!" The ghosts soon followed him out the door.

Jack looked at Allie. "Well, there's your truth." He said, not caring about Allie's torment anymore. "You can finally rest." Mayor Stine said. "Maybe I will." Allie smirked, looking at Jack, who desperately wanted to say "Oh you'll definitely rest" but kept his mouth shut. Allie looked up, seeing the night sky.

The townspeople began to leave the church, still murmuring. Allie, Jack, Elsa, and Monica stayed. Wendy semi-understood why and walked outside.

"After all these years. Well then." She reached out as if to touch Jack, but he took a step back. "Ok." Allie said softly. "I'll see you upstairs, Jack." Allie said as her spiritual form soon faded, she winked at Jack before she was fully gone.

"Wow. Embarrassed and proven wrong, she acts like nothing happened." Monica observed.

"Yeah, I don't think upstairs was the right word for her." Jack quipped.

Elsa approached Jack. "Are you ok?" "The truth is out. After all this time. It's finally out." Jack said as he looked at her. "How does it feel?" Elsa asked. Jack looked at her and smirked. "Uplifting." "Come on." Elsa said softly. The three walked out of the church, seeing a number of the townspeople interacting with the other spirits. Some were laughing, some were just nodded. One person tried to high five one of the spirits, only to hit the tree behind them.

"Well Jack Harvey." Wendy smirked as she approached. "It's been a long time."

"It sure has Wendy." He confirmed.

"Only took most of my life, but I guess I can finally see a ghost." Wendy joked.

"You certainly can honey!" Wendy looked behind her, her eyes shooting open. "And it's about time." Wendy's mouth dropped open in shock. Elsa stepped forward. "Grandma?" She asked.

"That's right." Wendy's mother, Kathleen, stepped out of the shadows, revealing her curly white hair and deep brown eyes. Clad in an angelic-esque white dress.

"You really are just like me." She said, sounding proud. "You've grown up so beautiful. It's amazing how much she looks like you Wendy." Wendy's eyes filled with tears; Elsa's eyes were no different. Jack's eyebrow arched, as if he finally saw the resemblance.

"Oh, come here." Kathleen pulled Wendy and Elsa into a hug.

Jack and Monica looked on. The trees started to shake with the wind, leaves fell down like snow.

"Mom," Wendy started. "Oh, dry your eyes." Kathleen said as she broke the hug. "I've known for a long time I had some unfinished business. I was just never sure what it was, most of us are never sure. But when you said, you could really use me," She paused again. "I knew my unfinished business was the two of you and they couldn't let me out fast enough." Kathleen explained.

"They?" Jack and Monica softly wondered.

"Although I'll admit, I could've handled it much better. I should've appeared to you earlier instead of just moving the picture." Kathleen noted, looking at Elsa. "Though I am surprised you didn't see me in the kitchen. I mean I was right there, sitting on the counter, when you two argued."

"Would've been a good place for you to step in." Elsa laughed.

Katherine looked embarrassed to say, "Yeah, I realize that now. I'm not very good at this ghost thing."

"You get used to it." Jack said.

"I'm used to being on the other side of ghostly conversations, Mr. Harvey." Kathleen chuckled. "I am so sorry, truly a bad decision on my part. By the way never yell at your mother like that again." Kathleen said.

"Wait, what about dad?" Wendy asked, taking the heat off Elsa. "Oh, you know your father. He's too lazy to take care of unfinished business." Kathleen joked.

"I'm just happy to finally see you come home and to see my granddaughter again." Kathleen said, cupping Elsa's face. "This town will be safer with you around darling. I don't ever want you to think of this as a curse, it's a gift. Remember that." Elsa wiped her eyes as Kathleen removed her hands.

"I will. I promise." Elsa said. "Good."

"Wait a second, were you part of those whispers?" Elsa asked, for she was no longer hearing them. Kathleen almost seemed puzzled and hesitant to answer, "Whispers? I don't recall those in my time. But things may have changed." That made Elsa feel more confused about them. "Now I must be off. I think I've kept your grandfather waiting long enough."

"Mom,"

"Don't you start again. I will always be here whenever you need me." Kathleen pointed to Wendy's heart. "Welcome home Wendy." Kathleen hugged Wendy one last time. "And Elsa, look out for your mother please." Kathleen chuckled. "Oh. I almost forgot. Mr. Harvey." Kathleen approached Jack slowly, "I believe you have someone waiting for you. He's been," She paused with a smirk. "Let's say clinging to me for a while. But he's still waiting on you to arrive." Jack knew without a shadow of a doubt who Kathleen meant. His eyes started to tear up and he smiled. "Thank you." He said. Kathleen smiled, then wrapped Jack in a hug. She whispered in his ear, "Thank you for helping my granddaughter."

"She helped me." He whispered back.

But Kathleen had something else to say. Whatever else she whispered in Jack's ear, it caused confusion to drive the happiness away from his face.

Kathleen stepped back and Jack looked at her. She winked, "You'll figure it out." She whispered before she started to ascend, soon vanishing into a white light that breached the night sky.

"What did she say?" Elsa asked. But Jack didn't answer, he stood in confusion until Monica nudged him.

"Huh? Oh, she thanked me for helping you. But she clearly got it wrong. No disrespect." Jack said. "None taken." Wendy said.

"Well, this has been quite the night." Monica joked. She wanted to change the subject.

"Can't argue with that." Jack said as he looked up to the sky, and Elsa noticed as she wiped the tears from her eyes.

"So, I guess this means it's time huh?" She asked. Jack knew what she meant. "I guess so." He looked back at her.

"Mainly because I know he's waiting for me." Jack wiped his eyes and chuckled a bit. "Thank you. I couldn't have done this without the two of you." Jack said, his eyes started to tear up again. Elsa walked up to Jack and hugged him. He hugged her back; she was lucky her hands didn't faze through him. "Thank you. For being my first human friend." Jack broke the hug, sniffled back his tears and his running nose. He looked over at Monica, who didn't hesitate to give him a small hug.

"Thank you." He chuckled. "I don't think I can thank you two enough. You two are truly the weirdest, but bravest people in Steeple Hills. Take care of this place." Jack said. "I'll send you a sign from the other side. A cloud shaped like a pumpkin feels right." He laughed as he started to ascend. "So long Jack." Elsa said softly. Monica waved. But

Jack wasn't the only one. Numerous other spirits hugged their loved ones goodbye before they ascended. A ghostly couple even danced into the sky as they vanished into the white light.

Jack got a look at his hometown, seeing its beauty for the last time. The light around him glowed bright green like the light of fireflies, vanishing into the night sky.

Monica stepped forward. "Hell, of a night huh Elsa." She said. "You got that right," Elsa put her arm on Monica's shoulder. "Partner." Wendy smiled, knowing Elsa had finally found a true friend.

✳✳✳

Little kids walked the streets, trick or treating. Wendy answered her door in a crimson robe with a purple hat. The house's porch was decorated from corner to corner. Monica and Elsa, however, sat inside Mel's Diner. Sitting across from each other in a booth. "You ready?" Monica asked. "Hope so." Elsa said.

Mel approached the table with a tray in his hands, while wearing a Captain America mask. Two plates of pumpkin pancakes and two large glasses. "Ok. Two pumpkin pancakes," He set the plates down, each one had three large pancakes stacked on them. "One pumpkin chocolate milkshake for you Monica." "Thanks Mel."

"And a pumpkin vanilla milkshake for you," Mel paused, "Elsa." She said. "Thank you." Mel said with a smile. "Thanks Mel." "Now do you two want some pumpkin whipped cream?" Elsa looked at Monica, who nodded with a big grin. Mel didn't even need to hear the words. He sprayed the milkshakes and the pancakes with pumpkin whip cream.

Elsa stared in surprise as the pumpkin whipped cream slunk down the edges of the glasses, and how it ran over the side of the pancakes.

"Enjoy and Happy Halloween!" Mel said happily as he walked away. "Thanks Mel." They said unintentionally simultaneously. Monica smirked looking at Elsa. "What?" She asked. "I'm waiting to see you take a bite." Monica said. Mel's pumpkin pancakes didn't need a knife, they cut like butter once Elsa's fork touched it, and the whipped cream just made them softer. She placed the piece of pancake in her mouth and the look of surprise overtook her face. "Oh my god." She said. "Yeah?" "This is delicious."
"I told you." Monica bit into her food, while Elsa took a sip of her milkshake. "Wow." She said. "So. What do you think of Steeple Hills now?" Monica asked, a slight chuckle in her voice. Elsa smiled, with a bit of a milk mustache on her face. "I think I'm starting to like it." Monica smiled and held her glass up, "Happy Halloween!" Elsa clinked her glass against Monica's,

"Happy Halloween!"

Elsa Carlyle will return!

The green light faded as Jack felt the cool night air. The sky was a mix of blue and purple. It was full of stars, but the moon was nowhere to be seen. Tombstones and headstones plagued the ground ahead of them. It wasn't the great beyond that Jack had expected.

"What the?" He was cut off by the sound of a whimper. One he hadn't heard in a long time. Jack look forward, seeing a black hound running across the graveyard. "BORIS!" Jack shouted with delight as Boris tackled him, licking his face repeatedly. "I missed you too!" Jack hugged the black hound. "I'm sorry it took me so long!" Boris licked his face; Jack knew this meant he had forgiven him. Boris whimpered again, then ran back the way he came.

"Boris?" Boris stopped and looked at Jack,

"Woof!"

(Come on!)

Boris barked and kept moving forward. Jack stood there confused, "Why did I understand that?" He ran after Boris. The graveyard looked like it could go on for miles as Jack followed Boris into a brewing fog. "Boris, wait up." Jack called; Boris stopped in his tracks. He let out a whimper as the fog thinned out, revealing a large stone building in the center of the graveyard. The stone was painted purple, the windows were tinted red, and the door was a bright green. "What is this place?" Jack wondered.

"Woof."

(Look down!)

"What?" Jack asked. But he got his answer as two lights kicked on brightly, nearly blinding Jack. Boris kept his head down for he had faced the lights before. The sudden light revealed a small courtyard with a broken wooden bench, but lush green grass. Boris wiped his paws on a black mat, then nudged the door open. Though he was puzzled, and mesmerized by this new world around him, Jack followed Boris inside. An intoxicating smell caught their nostrils as the door closed behind them. It was so strong that Boris covered his nose and whimpered. Jack took a whiff, "Smells like hot wings." The lights turned on with every step they took. Boris jumped onto the nearest bench as Jack looked around the room. "Wait. How are we in Grand Central Station?" He asked in a whisper.

"You're not! Well, you are. But you're also not!" A voice said, its echo boomed like thunder throughout the empty concourse. It sounded like someone who had the microphone too close to their mouth. Jack looked around but saw no one. Boris didn't move.

"Over here Mr. Harvey." Jack stopped spinning, seeing a tall man with messy silver hair standing atop the staircase. He wore tight black leather pants and a collared purple shirt. "It's about time you arrived. Apologies for the delay. There was a," The man paused. "You know what? Let's call it an other-worldly clerical error for the time being. I'm still trying to figure it out." He was a bit long in the face. Boris growled then hopped off the bench. He clung to Jack's side like a fly to honey. "Oh, no need to growl at me Boris. You know me. Actually, that might be why you're growling. Sorry for the boom. I couldn't help myself." The man chuckled.
"How do you know-"

"All will be answered soon enough Jack my boy. Let's start off with this, my name is Zhane. Welcome to the Hereafter. I feel you and I will have a lot to discuss."
"Such as?" Jack asked.

"Well for starters, why it took you twenty-five years to arrive."

"Is that why I'm here? That wasn't my fault." Jack argued.

"Oh, I'm well aware, don't you worry. This isn't some kind of punishment." Zhane said.

"Woof!"

(That's debatable!)

Zhane waved Boris off, which Jack didn't like.

"But why am I, scratch that. Why are WE here then?"

"Now that question I can answer. It's actually quite simple, well simple-ish. It depends on your interpretation." Jack didn't like the sound of that, and his face showed it.

"You and Boris are here because, well to be blunt.... You two have some unfinished business."

Jack Harvey will return!